RAT LIFE

TEDD ARNOLD

SLEUTH
D I A L

DIAL BOOKS
A member of Penguin Group (USA) Inc.
Published by The Penguin Group
Penguin Group (USA) Inc.
375 Hudson Street
New York, NY 10014, U.S.A.

Penguin Group (Canada), 90 Eglinton Avenue East, Suite 700, Toronto, Ontario, Canada M4P 2Y3 (a division of Pearson Penguin Canada Inc.) • Penguin Books Ltd, 80 Strand, London WC2R 0RL, England • Penguin Ireland, 25 St. Stephen's Green, Dublin 2, Ireland (a division of Penguin Books Ltd) • Penguin Group (Australia), 250 Camberwell Road, Camberwell, Victoria 3124, Australia (a division of Pearson Australia Group Pty Ltd) • Penguin Books India Pvt Ltd, 11 Community Centre, Panchsheel Park, New Delhi - 110 017, India • Penguin Group (NZ), Cnr Airborne and Rosedale Roads, Albany, Auckland 1310, New Zealand (a division of Pearson New Zealand Ltd) • Penguin Books (South Africa) (Pty) Ltd, 24 Sturdee Avenue, Rosebank, Johannesburg 2196, South Africa • Penguin Books Ltd, Registered Offices: 80 Strand, London WC2R 0RL, England

Designed by Nancy R. Leo-Kelly
Text set in Century Schoolbook
Printed in the U.S.A.
3 5 7 9 10 8 6 4 2

Library of Congress Cataloging-in-Publication Data
Arnold, Tedd.
Rat life / Tedd Arnold.
p.   cm.
Summary: After developing an unusual friendship with a young Vietnam War veteran in 1972, fourteen-year-old Todd discovers his writing talent and solves a murder mystery.
ISBN-13: 978-0-8037-3020-5
[1. Creative writing—Fiction. 2. Vietnam War, 1961–1975—Veterans—Fiction. 3. Mystery and detective stories.] I. Title.
PZ7.A7379Rat 2007   [Fic]—dc22   2006018429

To Mary Jane Auch, Patience Brewster, Bruce Coville, Cynthia DeFelice, Robin Pulver, Vivian Vande Velde, and Ellen Stoll Walsh—fantastically talented writers without whose enthusiastic encouragement and critical commentary this book would have never happened.

And to Lauri Hornik, my fine and trusting editor, willing to take a giant leap of faith on a first novel.

A list of possible first lines:

1. A dead guy washed up from the river.

I think a dead guy showing up is always a great way to start a story. I mean, if that was the first line I read in a book, I'd keep reading. Wouldn't you? But someone said, when you're brainstorming, you should never stop with your first idea. Maybe I can come up with something better.

2. Where I live there are twenty-four beds. I have to make twenty-two of them.

That's a riddle I made up a while ago. Followed by the question "So where do I live?" When you give up, I say, "In a motel. Get it?" But when I read it objectively, like it's some stranger's words, it sounds like he's a big whiner.

3. The truth is, this first line you're reading is the last thing I wrote.

Interesting, in a boring, dorkish way. Like it's some big secret that writers sometimes write things out of order. Then shuffle the pieces together. My English teacher said a strong first line catches the reader's interest. So, now that I'm finished writing everything else, it's time to write the first line. Wait. Does this give away the ending—that I survived?

4. To whom it may concern.

Just because I never saw other authors use this opening line doesn't mean it's a bad idea. But it sounds like the beginning of a suicide note. Which this definitely is not. Besides, it's probably the only phrase I know where I'm sure I used the word *whom* correctly. That might set the standards for grammar way too high too early.

5. I'm stupid.

Okay, true. But I should save that for the title of my autobiography.

6. "I wish you hadn't come here."

Maybe that's where I should start, with Rat behind me, speaking so low, I almost didn't hear him over the pounding in my ears. Even so, his voice scared the crap out of me. After that opening line, the rest would go like—

```
I whirled around. Rat held a rifle,
pointed vaguely at my knees. He didn't
meet my gaze but looked past me, at
the porch, the screen door. "You gotta
come with me." I searched his face for a
sign, desperate to believe that this was
some kind of joke. He lifted the rifle,
swung the barrel until it pointed to the
woods. "This way."
```

```
I had to agree with him. I wished I
hadn't come. What was I thinking?
```

Yeah. What was I thinking? I ask myself that a lot. But then again, I can't think of a single thing that I seriously wish I had done differently. Except for the pup. That's when this started. The day I found the pup. That's when I first met Rat, even though I didn't know who he was yet.

But, I don't know. Starting out like that—in the middle of a scary part? It sounds kinda like the stuff they put on the back covers of cheesy paperbacks. Try to suck people into buying the books. It must work, or they wouldn't do it. But still . . .

Maybe this first-line thing isn't working out so well. I'll give it about two more minutes.

One more minute.

Wait, what about—

```
7. Ann Carpenter went to the movies with
me wearing a bikini.
```

Just kidding. Besides, it's screwed up. Sounds like I'm the one wearing the bikini. I meant to say—

```
7a. Ann Carpenter wore a bikini with me
to the movies.
```

That's not right either. But like I said, just kidding.

Thirty seconds.

Ten.

Five.

Look, just forget the first line. Either you read it like I wrote it or you don't. I can't help it.

1

"I'll take that, Todd!"

I looked up. Mrs. Hagerwood was beside me. She reached down and pulled the notebook from under my hand. The spiral wire made a zipping sound against my pencil point. Snapped it off. The bell rang. My face got hot as I stood. Trailing the crowd of fleeing kids out the door, I glanced back. She was reading it!

Leaky waited in the hall beaming with glee over my impending doom. "Wha'd she get?"

"Nothing!" I kept going.

"No. I mean . . . was it something I already read? Or what?" There was real concern in his voice.

"I *just* wrote it," I said, not slowing down.

"Far out!" he called to my back. "Was I in it?"

"For about half a second. Then you got vaporized."

"You killed me off?" He croaked dramatically, but I was around the corner and gone.

History was my last class. What a drag. Mr. Bailey's idea of teaching? Collect homework, give a quiz, then read a forty-minute lecture from a thick binder while we take notes that are graded. Homework was always, "Outline the next chapter." I preferred learning history from movies.

The really crazy part? All the stuff every day in the news? For Bailey, none of it was happening. Like the Vietnam thing. Or that presidential candidate, George Wallace, getting shot. Not Bailey's concern.

Last bell of the day ended the torture. I returned a library book. At the gym I signed up for summer tennis. When I got to my locker the halls were quiet. I shouldered my backpack. Passed by Mrs. Hagerwood's room. Her door was open but the lights were out. On the desk where I always sat was my notebook. Weird. I leaned into the room. No one home. I slipped in, stuffed the notebook in my pack, and left.

At the bike rack behind the gym I dialed my combination lock. Behind me I heard, "He-e-ey, Toddler! Why do you even bother locking that chunk-o-rust?" It was Leaky on his new ten-speed. Before I could deliver a cutting reply, he added, "So how'd you kill me this time?"

"You can read it yourself. I got it back."

"Cool. Lemme see."

"Not now. I gotta go." I popped the lock and wrapped the chain around the seat post.

"Hey, you hear about the dead guy?"

"Look, man, I gotta go." I threw my leg over the bike.

"This ain't a joke!"

"Okay, so tell me."

"Coach said he heard it on the radio at lunch. Guy washed up outta the river."

"Where'd they find him?" I remembered seeing something that morning on the way to school. Passing the turn-off to Fischer's Bridge I caught a glimpse of cop cars and flashing lights down by the river. I didn't stop. It would have made me late.

Leaky shrugged. "That's all Coach said. You know him— being 'motivational.' Trying to get us to work on our swimming skills this summer." I shoved off, but Leaky yelled after me, "You can put that dead guy in a story maybe."

―――――――――

Home was a long ride from school. Water Street was quickest. But I preferred going down along the river.

The Chemanga River, where it flows through town, is walled in on both sides by levees. The sloped, grassy dikes are maybe ten feet high—six feet wide at the top. On my side of the river you could walk or bike the levee all the way out of town to where it stopped at Fischer's Bridge. In places, the river snakes away from the levee, and the land between is a flat flood plain of tall grass with random clumps of thick woods sometimes growing right to the water's edge. The meadows and woods are laced with trails. I love riding down by the river and disappearing for a while.

I rode down to one particular spot, a tiny clearing on the bank, concealed by trees and weeds. Great for when you want to be alone. I was thinking about Leaky's news. What would it be like to find a body sloshing on shore?

Gross! But what if I found he had scratched his murderer's name in the mud? I'd be a hero! Might get a reward! I could buy a new bike.

No such luck today.

Once in a while strange things do show up in the river. Last month I hauled in a section of Formica countertop. I set it on some rocks, a makeshift bench up off the mud.

I sat on my bench now and pulled out the notebook.

In the last couple years I'd written a lot of stupid things—about aliens and spies and all. Mostly I tried to be funny. Once I read one to Leaky and Brian. They thought it was cool. Started suggesting things to write about. Leaky began a list of gross facts to include in my stories, "to juice 'em up."

The guys actually *wanted* to read my stuff. I admit—it felt good. I started trying to impress them. Worked harder on the words. Sometimes rewrote whole pages to clean up all the cross-outs.

No teacher had ever gotten hold of one. Until now.

Mrs. Haggleword didn't realize she had less than a minute to live. She was too busy giving me a hard time, as usual.

"But . . ." I pleaded.

"No buts, young man! Sit down or walk to the office."

I looked at my feet. When had I stood up? I looked out the window again. From my desk at the back corner of the room, I had a view out the high bank of windows all the way to the gym.

"Helicopter" came to mind, because my brain refused to accept "spaceship." But this wasn't some noisy chopper dropping Marines into the jungle. Without a prop, it hovered at second-floor level in perfect silence, getting closer. Soon it would be in full view. Then my classmates would know—I was trying to save them! I pointed again and pleaded, "Mrs. Haggleword, just look out the win—"

"Okay, mister. To the office!"

She stood pointing at the door, me pointing at the window. I dropped my arm. What could I do? Sidestepping across the back of the room, I kept one eye on Mrs. Haggleword, one eye on the window. My leg knocked the corner of a table. Tattered copies of Fahrenheit 451 cascaded to the floor. Leaky ducked low and made faces at me over his shoulder.

The unearthly craft arrived at our windows, in

full view if anyone turned to look. But all eyes were on me. I opened the door enough to slip into the hall. I looked back. Leaky made a comical toodle-oo wave. Haggleword's glare commanded me to shut the door. Fingertips on the knob, I began to ease it closed when I was hit by a roar like the amplified static at a rock concert. Blinding whiteness filled the classroom. I had to look away. Hot light blazed into the hall through the gap in the doorway.

As quickly as it had come, the noise and light vanished. The suddenness made me dizzy. The doorknob was so hot that I jerked my hand away. Where light had beamed across my wrist, a red, blistered stripe glowed like a bad sunburn.

I eased the door open with my toe. Trails of smoke followed its outward swing. I stepped back into the room that I had just left—what—five? ten seconds ago? Outside, the hovering ship was gone. Thick smoke escaped through a gaping hole where windows had been. Melted glass oozed down the blackened wall like syrup. The pile of Fahrenheit 451 paperbacks quietly burned. Metal parts of the desks sagged into molten pools. Where each of my classmates had been sitting, there was a pile of ashes. The largest pile was beside the remains of Mrs. Haggleword's desk. A breeze blew in and swirled her ashes into a tiny tornado.

2.

I held the notebook on my lap. Hesitated before opening it. The way I portrayed Mrs. Hagerwood in my story was just for a laugh—for Leaky and the guys. Actually, I thought she was okay. Knowing she had read it made me nervous about reading it again and seeing it through her eyes. Good thing there was nothing else in there—just my story on the first few pages.

Wait. There was something else! I flipped to the last page. My cartoon of Mr. Bailey holding his fat belly under a sign that read "Maternity Ward."

Had Hagerwood seen this? My face lit up with the heat of a blush. Unbelievable! All alone in the woods and I'm blushing!

Wait! Something else!

I thumbed back another page. My cartoon fantasy of Ann Carpenter in a bikini. Had she seen this too? Can you die from blushing?

I flipped to the front, to my story. Red markings. She graded it? Above the first sentence, Mrs. Hagerwood had written, "Great opening line! You grabbed my interest right away." I read that twice to be sure I hadn't misunderstood.

Next, she had circled *Haggleword* with a comment in the margin, "Amusing word-play, but a bit juvenile for my taste."

I couldn't believe what I was reading! There was more, but I skipped to the last page. Where the copies of *Fahrenheit 451* were burning she had written, "Nice ironic detail."

The last line, penciled just before she snatched it from my desk, was "A breeze blew in through the open window and swirled her ashes into a tiny tornado."

Oh, geez! Did she really read that?

Below she had written, "Not to haggle over words, mind you, but I call those knee-high tornadoes 'dust devils.'"

It was weird—her comments. As if she took the story . . . seriously.

Could she have actually liked my writing?

I stood up. What time was it? I had beds to make! I crammed the notebook into my pack. Dug out my transistor radio, found Creedence Clearwater singing "Who'll Stop the Rain." Stuck it in my shirt pocket, shouldered my pack, and biked back onto Water Street.

Living at a motel is not my idea of a good idea. But if we *had* to, why not in Hawaii? At least Florida. Anywhere but Elmore, New York. Oak Acres Court is out of town, a couple miles past where Water Street becomes Highway 254. It's the kind of motel with a row of little cabins. The office sits out front, a separate building by the driveway entrance. We live in the office. More precisely, the office is where the living room would be in a normal house.

Dad worked nights at the glass factory and slept days. Mom ran the motel. I made beds, cleaned floors, and helped with laundry. For free! Because I had the last dad on earth who didn't believe in allowance. My work was, according to Dad, my "contribution to the family business." And right now, the family business had beds to be made.

At the edge of town I couldn't resist a quick detour down to Fischer's Bridge. Yellow police tape was tied to the bridge railing and encircled maybe twenty yards of the near shoreline. I could see tire tracks through some weeds down near the water, but nothing else. What did I expect? The impression of a body in the mud like some dark snow angel? I didn't stick around.

Past the turnoff to Fischer's Bridge is a stretch of open road running along the river. "Who'll Stop the Rain" was followed by Derek and the Dominoes—Eric Clapton—doing "Layla." I let go of the handlebars, leaned back, and played air guitar.

She likes my writing!

3

I saw something up ahead. On the far side of the road, a dog—no, a pup—was trotting along the gravel shoulder coming my way. I swerved across to the pup's side of the road. It spotted me and abruptly sat down. Looked over its shoulder uncertainly, then back at me. Scratched with a hind leg, yawned, then seemed to just wait. I slowed to a stop about thirty feet away, careful not to scare it. Turned my radio down.

"Hey, fella!" I said. Its short, pointed tail started wagging. I leaned my bike against the guardrail and walked slowly toward the pup. "Com'ere, little guy."

That got its whole body wagging. It stood up halfway, trying to decide, wanting to trust me. Luckily there was no traffic to disrupt the moment.

"That's it. Come to Papa."

Finally, when I was five feet away, it took a couple shy steps toward me. As I reached out, it hunkered down, rolled over, and showed me a round, pink belly. Her tail—I could now see it was a she—did a windshield wiper thing in the dirt. I stroked her tummy and she piddled all over herself. She scrambled to her feet and jumped at my face. I laughed and scooped her up. Every part of her was in excited motion, all wiggles and sloppy kisses as I walked back to my bike. Her spotted white fur was sun-warmed and dusty.

"Where do you belong, girl?" I said, scratching behind her ears. Back toward town I saw only the small speck of a guy on a bike. There were houses back there and houses farther out where I was headed. But none right here. This pup was in the middle of nowhere.

"Whatcha wanna do, girl?" I gazed down the road. A truck appeared in the distance, heading toward us into town. I murmured singsong things to the pup, wondering what to do.

It was a cement truck coming, getting louder. The pup suddenly pricked up her ears and turned toward the noise.

"It's okay," I said. "Let's go home now." I figured there was nothing else to do but carry her with me—somehow. Maybe in my backpack while I walked my bike. I'd find her owners later.

The truck was close now. I stepped back but couldn't get far. The backs of my legs were against the guardrail. The pup started to squirm in my arms, trying to get away. The truck roared toward us. She got frantic. She squirmed and pawed at me. Her butt popped out below my arms. She yipped as I struggled to scoop her back up.

Then the huge truck was right there. The noise covered everything. The pup cried out but I barely heard. She twisted. Clawed madly for escape. Sank her teeth into my arm. Needle-sharp puppy teeth. It startled me. I let loose. Just a little. Just for a second.

She sprang away. Toward the road. I fumbled for her. Somehow, that propelled her farther.

No! The wheels!

She tumbled. Hit the road. Scrambled for her feet.

Under the wheels. A small thump. Added to an avalanche of noise.

"NO-O-O-O!"

And the truck was past. Dust and leaves trailing. Me, frozen, still reaching.

Yipping emerged from the retreating roar. There was grit in my eyes. Hard to see clearly. The pup was struggling.

No. I mean, part of the pup was struggling. She cried a continuous, yipping wail. Her hind legs were pressed flat against the asphalt. And twisted backwards. Behind her head.

And she cried! She cried and cried!

I dropped to my knees. A tiny trickle of blood from her nose. A little red in one eye. That was all. But-oh-my-god-her-legs. Her back.

How can you still be alive?

"Oh, baby," I groaned softly. It just slipped out. I'd never called anyone or anything "baby" in my life. I wanted someone to tell me this wasn't my life. Tell me I didn't have to see this.

Tell me I didn't let go.

Her crying drilled into my skull. I couldn't think. I couldn't see clearly. What was the matter with my damn eyes?

"That dog needs killing," said a voice.

I looked up, uncomprehending. "What . . . ?" Someone on the far side of the road. Guy on a bike.

"Dog needs killing," he said again. "Too bad my uncle ain't here. He'd enjoy doing it."

"WHAT?" I screamed, suddenly reduced to a one-word vocabulary.

He shrugged and rode away. I was alone again, faced with more pain than I had ever witnessed in my life.

4

Coming home on a normal school day, I would take my bike behind the office and lock it to the iron handrail of our back-door steps. On a normal day I would head for the drink machine outside the office door. Wouldn't even need coins. Would pull the key from my pocket, open it up, and "swallow a bottle of profits," as Dad would say.

But that day . . . that day I dropped my bike against the drink machine and went straight to my room. Slammed the door.

Mom never missed much, no matter where she was on the motel grounds. For one thing, I was late. She'd probably been watching for me. And I'd left my bike where it would be in the way of customers. It didn't take her two minutes before she tapped on my bedroom door. When she got no reply, she came in anyway. Found me with my back to her, staring into the dresser mirror at my wet, streaked face and bloody shirt and arms.

"Todd, what's wrong?" she asked. I didn't answer. "Todd?" She came around in front of me. Saw the blood.

"Oh, baby," she whispered.

5

"Rabies?" The word croaked out as if I hadn't used my voice in years. "You think . . . ?" But I couldn't finish.

The emergency room doctor was examining the bite. He sniffed it. "Bourbon," he said, smiling at my mother.

She wasn't in the mood for smiles. "We were out of medicinal alcohol. I washed it with soap and Southern Comfort."

"Good choice," he said and winked at me. Then he was all business. "So tell me everything."

I shrugged. Like it was simple. "Found a pup by the river. I tried to pick it up. It bit me . . . and got away."

I had given that same *Reader's Digest* condensed version to Mom back in my bedroom. That's when she had gone into her no-nonsense mode. Cleaned my arm. Called Dad. Switched on the "No Vacancy" sign and locked the office. Got Gramma Gram out of Cabin 1 and helped her into the backseat of the car. On the drive to the hospital, Mom asked more questions. I gave her "I don't know" answers. She must have wondered how a bite from a pup got me so dirty. And how did a bite that didn't look so bad once it was cleaned up leave so much blood on my shirt?

But questions from the doctor had to be answered.

"Okay, then," he said as he cleaned my arm all over again. "Tell me about the dog."

"A pup!" I corrected him angrily. He and Mom both looked at me, startled. "Just a pup," I repeated, quieter.

Eventually he prodded out of me the pup's size, how much I thought it weighed, how clean it was, if it had acted normally, if it had any sores or injuries on its body.

Mom listened to everything, even though her attention was divided. She kept one eye on Gramma Gram, who sat in a nearby chair. Gram was repeatedly taking everything out of her purse, piling it in her lap, then putting it all back.

When the doctor finished, he wrapped the bite area with gauze, taped the edges, then folded his arms.

"Here's the deal," he said. "In a minute I'll give you a shot in the arm to prevent infection. And a prescription for antibiotics. Your arm will hurt for a couple days. A pup's milk teeth aren't big, but they're sharp. It got you good." He glanced at a paper for my name. "Todd, you need to try and find the pup. If it's healthy and free of rabies, then so are you. Let's see. Today's Thursday? I'll give you until Monday."

"Find it?" I stared at him. He had to be kidding. "What if I . . . can't?"

"Well," he said, "the rabies vaccination is a series of fourteen shots. Right here." He lightly poked my stomach with his finger. "It's not fun. Try to find that pup."

Friday morning. I felt like I hadn't slept. My arm had throbbed all night as I slipped in and out of weird dreams. On most mornings, some motel customers were gone at the crack of dawn. I would change those beds before school. Not today. The clock said I was already going to be late for homeroom.

Mom heard me in the bathroom. "I turned off your alarm," she said from the other side of the door. "I thought you should stay home today." Normally, those words would have seemed heaven-sent. But I knew if I stayed she would want to talk. Ask questions.

"I'm okay," I answered. "Plus, I have a history test."

"You always have a history test. Why don't you rest today."

"I'm okay!" I yelled as I jerked open the bathroom door. Pack already on my shoulder, I squeezed by her. In the kitchen I picked up a banana. The morning newspaper was spread on the table. Mom's cup of coffee sat beside the headline: "Body Found in Chemanga River." I wanted to read the article but didn't dare slow down. Mom was just seconds away from insisting I stay.

It was a long, long day. I spent most of the time wishing I had taken Mom's advice. No one noticed my bandaged arm because I wore a long-sleeved shirt. Leaky gave me a hard time about leaving my spaceship story at home. "I get vaporized and you forget about it?" he whined.

Most of Hagerwood's class was normal—wrapping things up before reviewing for the final exam. Then, minutes before the bell, she changed things on us. No big surprise, really, for her. Mrs. Hagerwood was one of those spontaneous-type teachers. You could almost guess it by looking at her. Long hair. Strings of beads. At the beginning of the school year, Dad met her at open house. On the way home he had grumbled about "letting hippies teach our children."

But I liked her class. In little ways, she made English interesting. Even something stupid like diagramming sentences? She had us do sentences like: "I never let my schooling get in the way of my education." A Mark Twain quote. She was cool.

She said to the class, "I don't normally give much written homework on weekends. But . . ."

Everyone groaned.

"But," she persisted, "we still have some time before summer." She hesitated and glanced at me. "We've covered the required material. With a little review, I'm satisfied you'll be ready for the final. However, looking back over the year, one thing we haven't spent enough time on . . ."

Another darting glance my way. What was going on?

". . . what we could all use more work on . . ."

She was looking straight at me now!

". . . is creative writing."

Oh, geez! I put my head down on the desk.

This was all my fault.

Before leaving school, I went to the main office. Called home.

"Oak Acres Court," Mom answered.

"Hey, it's me."

"Todd, honey. Are you okay?"

"Yeah, no sweat. Look, I was just wondering . . . if things are under control there, I thought . . . I'd stop at some houses on the way home. Try to find the pup." Not quite true. I wanted to find the owners. Let them know what happened. Also I needed to ask them if the pup ever had its rabies shots.

"Good idea, hon," she said. "Need help with that?"

"No! That's okay," I answered quickly. "Thanks, Mom."

Before I got out of town to where IT happened, I started knocking on doors. I went to dozens of houses. Found houses behind houses, streets I'd never seen before. Up one dirt road I found a full-sized canvas teepee with a hairy woman and an even hairier man gardening. They weren't missing a pup.

I came to a construction site, a future mini-market. I rode up to where the foundations were taking shape. It was pointless, but for the record I asked one of the crew anyway. He was telling me he knew nothing about a stray pup when I heard a familiar roar behind me. A cement truck pulled in from the highway. I almost puked.

That night, when Mom changed my bandage, there was no sign of infection. She didn't ask any questions. But I knew by her silence—she was waiting for me to talk. I couldn't.

I had trouble sleeping again. In the middle of the night I was awakened by a pulsing pain. Found I was lying on my arm. I rolled over, but the rest of the night was jumbled with dreams—of me holding the pup and letting it go. The moment replayed dozens of times and each time I tried to not let go and each time the bite was a surprise. And each time . . .

7

Saturday morning, I changed beds and hauled laundry until ten, then asked Mom if I could finish after lunch. Said I needed to keep looking for the pup.

I started toward town hoping to catch some people who hadn't been home yesterday. But I remembered that the pup had been headed *into* town. Maybe it came from farther out. I turned around.

Past our motel was a gas station followed by a dozen or more houses with their backs to the river. Then the occasional ramshackle car repair shop, and a couple junk-filled barns. Finally the drive-in theater. No luck anywhere. It was dawning on me that the pup had probably been dumped by some creep who simply didn't want the hassle. The unthinkable—taking fourteen rabies shots in the gut—was becoming a horrible possibility. I turned into the theater driveway and stopped for a breather before heading home.

I had been to the drive-in before. At night. But in daylight the place looked abandoned. It was open, though. The marquee announced: "ToNITE—2 CLINT

EASTWOODs—*Dirty Harry* PLUS *Play Misty for Me.*"

I was about to head home when I spotted a small house. It was beside the theater, but set way back off the road, so overgrown with trees and bushes that, driving by, you might not see it at all. I was a long way from where I had found the pup, but it couldn't hurt to ask.

A weedy gravel driveway angled off from the theater's entrance. I followed it downhill under a canopy of trees and stopped by the house. Leaned my bike against a porch post where an old tire also leaned, holding a pool of scummy water.

"Anybody home?" I called to the screen door. I stepped onto the porch. The inner door hung open, but it was completely dark inside. I knocked. Waited. Knocked again. "Anyone there?"

A long pause, then, "Who wants to know?" An unfriendly voice from the darkness inside.

"I was just . . . wondering," I spoke louder, haltingly, a little nervous about the place—and the voice. "I . . . uh . . . are you . . . missing a pup? I found one . . . well, I . . . I know where one is." Without a face to talk to, I had turned sideways to the door, looking and gesturing vaguely toward the highway.

"It's you," said the voice, low, and suddenly so close, I jumped. Standing behind the screen, a guy squinted out at me. "Did you do it?"

"What?" I backed up without looking and stepped right off the porch, awkwardly catching my balance, one foot off, one foot on.

"You kill that dog?" He pushed the screen door open and stepped out. I pulled my other foot off the porch.

It was the guy I had seen on the bike. His gaze was tired looking but unblinking. "Yeah," he said, "you did." He took another step. The door slapped shut behind him. He was pale with short dark hair sticking up randomly. Wore only a T-shirt and green boxers. Not much taller than me. And in the light he didn't look much older. Except for his eyes.

I grabbed my bike. "I don't know what you're—"

"It had to be done," he said, low, quiet. For the first time there was feeling in his voice. "Dog had to be put down."

"It was a pup!" I said through my teeth. But I didn't even want to say that much. I pushed my bike back toward the driveway.

"Think a pup's too young to die?" he asked.

"Just shut up!" I yelled without stopping.

"I'm sorry." He spoke louder, my back to him. "What I said that day? About my uncle? That was uncalled for."

I had thrown my leg over the bike. I didn't push off, but I didn't turn around either.

"You did a hard thing," he said. "Did what you had to do."

I sat and stared at my handlebars like I couldn't remember what they were for. Then I looked uphill through the trees and underbrush. I could see an edge of highway. "You don't even know," I said aloud, but to myself, like I was daydreaming.

"I do know." He was beside my bike. I hadn't heard him come. "I saw you pick it up. Saw it get away. I was behind you, just toolin' home like you were. Hell, man, it coulda been me picking up that pup."

"But it *wasn't* you!" I replied angrily.

"Yeah, well . . ." The corner of his mouth twitched. "Luck of the draw, sometimes."

"Look! You're not missing a pup, right? So, I gotta go."

"Hey, wait," he said.

I pushed off.

"I wanna ask you something . . ."

I stood on the pedals, gaining speed uphill.

"You want a job?" he yelled. "Here at the drive-in?"

I kept going. Up and out onto the sunlit asphalt of the theater entrance.

"Free movies," I heard him shout.

I stopped pedaling, coasted in a wide circle, returned to the top of his driveway. When the guy saw me, a lopsided grin broke across his face and he added, "Free popcorn."

What with school and Dad working nights, Saturday lunches were one of the few times we all sat down together. With a week's worth of issues to catch up on, it could get tense. Like now. Dad was doing his usual best to clarify my request—to boil it down to the essentials, he would say. Which, if he opposed the request, often meant recasting it in the worst possible light.

"You want to work for a man named Rat?"

There were three things wrong with Dad's one simple sentence.

"His name isn't Rat," I said. "That's a nickname. And I didn't say I'd be working *for* Rat. I'll be working for the manager, Mr. Huber. And Rat, he's not . . . I mean, he's just a kid. A little older than me, I guess, but still. He just works there. With his mom."

Oops. Wrong thing to say! "And what about helping *your* mother *here*?" With Dad, no matter what I wanted, The Motel came first. If you asked me, it owned us more than we owned it.

"I can do both," I said, figuring I could worry about

the details later. "I *need* a job. My bike's a piece of crap." Dad's expression darkened at my language, but I was getting mad. "I never have enough money! Other kids get an allowance."

I had come back from the drive-in and asked Mom about the job while Dad was still asleep. So I knew it was okay with her as long as I did my schoolwork and motel chores. "But you still need to talk to your father," she had concluded.

Now he looked at her questioningly.

She shrugged. "I don't see why he can't give it a try."

"It'll only be weekends," I jumped in, "until school's out. Then I'll know more about how many hours I can handle."

"If you're worried about what *I* need," Mom said to Dad, "the bigger issue right now is Gram."

Whoa! I sat back. That was a big-time change of subject. I realized Mom was running interference for me.

Lately at our table, all other conversation paled beside the hot topic of caring for Dad's mother. Gramma Gram was getting worse, and Dad couldn't bear to put her in a nursing home. We all took turns keeping her company and helping feed her. But it was Mom who handled what Dad called "all the female things" that he couldn't deal with. When Mom mentioned Gram, that was my signal to clear out. Believe me, doing beds, laundry—even homework— was better than sitting through *that* painful discussion again.

Yes! I've-got-the-job-thank-you-Mom!

I put my plate in the sink and escaped to restock the drink machine. Then I picked up litter and carried it out back. In the trash bin I spotted yesterday's paper with the article about the dead guy in the river. The write-up didn't say much. An unidentified man found at Fischer's Bridge. The cause of death was "under investigation." One policeman interviewed admitted he was no expert but said the man was roughly mid-thirties, and had been in the river well over a week.

Back in fifth grade I did a big report about the river and its history. Since then I still saved stuff about it. Habit, I guess. Besides, I loved the river. It figured into some of my stories. So I tore out the article and stuffed it in my pocket.

Mom called me to get Gram's lunch. I carried it across the driveway to her cabin. She had lived with us at the motel since Gramps died. Two years now. By her door I set the plate on a small TV tray between two lawn chairs. That's where Gram liked to eat and where I read to her.

I gently knocked. "Gram?" I let myself in. "I have your lunch, Gram."

"Where . . . exactly?" she asked, standing up from the couch.

"Let's eat outside," I said, leading her gently. From her dresser I picked up my paperback of *Huckleberry Finn,* the book I was reading aloud to her.

After three steps she stopped. "Are we there yet?"

"Through this door," I answered.

Looking up as if seeing me for the first time, she said, "Well, aren't you a big . . ." She hesitated, searching for a word, then found one. ". . . camel."

9

Maybe if Dad believed in giving an allowance, I wouldn't have needed a job. I never had enough money. Years ago, Dad had a brilliant idea. He gave me the drink machine. It was so old, the local distributor no longer serviced it. Dad's deal was, "You buy the merchandise and return the empty bottles. And you keep the profits."

He handed me the key and added, "Let me show you something." He pulled the heavy machine away from the wall. It scraped dryly over the sidewalk. Bottles chinked inside. "See the back?"

I saw spiderwebs, dead bugs, dry leaves, and the power cord. Some mechanical guts showed down at the bottom, but rusted sheet metal covered most of the backside. Near the middle, about chest high, three round, jagged-edged holes poked outward. They were plugged with steel wool.

"Bullet holes," Dad said, pushing the machine back in place. That gave me a jolt. "Somebody din't git their sodee-pop." Dad always delivered what he considered his greatest wisdom in the voice of Jed Clampett from *The Beverly Hillbillies.*

"Cool," was all I could think to say.

"Ri-i-i-ight," he drawled. "Jus' keep yore customers satisfied."

I rubbed my hand over the smooth front of the machine. If something catches my interest, I get totally into it. Like I did with the river when we moved to Elmore. I explored it, drew maps, fished, and did that school project. So when Dad gave me the key to the drink machine, it became my new passion. The drink machine was all mine. My business. My kingdom!

My money!

I unlocked and pulled open the front and found where the bullet holes had been patched. Dad had set me up with a machine full of drinks and a change dispenser full of coins. I began figuring out how the machine worked. By evening, after fiddling with everything, I had learned the tricky part, the business part—how to reset the machine to raise the price. Hey, I needed the money! Who was gonna notice?

Next afternoon, I raced home from school, eager to see how much my gold mine had made on the first day of business. I found a sign taped over the coin slot. "Out of Order." Mom was just coming from a cabin with an armload of laundry.

"What happened?" I said, fumbling in my pocket for the key.

"I don't know, hon. After the third person couldn't get their drink I put a stop to it."

I saw the problem as soon as I'd peeled off Mom's sign.

The price above the coin slot still said fifteen cents.

What an idiot! I slapped the machine. Then posted my new price—twenty-five cents. That evening I watched from across the driveway. My first customers were two hippie-looking girls. One pointed at the price and yelled, "Rip-off!" The other looked around like they had to be on *Candid Camera* or something. They spotted the gas station down the road, where I knew two machines offered fifteen-cent drinks. Stunned, I watched them go, one of them ranting, "What kind of capitalist-pig head-trips are these motel people into?"

Truly Gross Facts (for Todd) (These are all true, man!)

by Lee Simmons

—Microscopic bugs live in your eyelashes and eat dead skin.

—20% of all "intestinal flatus" (that's fart gas, Todd) exits your body through your mouth.

—A male housefly, to attract a female, will offer a piece of rotten meat wrapped in a frothy coating of his own butt "secretions."

—Dead bodies that are buried improperly can turn into soap.

—On the island of Java, ratlike animals called Luaks often eat the ripest coffee beans. Farmers collect Luak "droppings," roast them, and make what they say is the best coffee in the world. (Hey Toddler—wake up and smell the Luak!)

—Some Buddhist yogis did tongue-lengthening stuff until they could lick their own eyebrows.

(Good story ideas, right? Lots more to come! The library has all these cool facts!!!)

10

Dad was outside fixing the lawn mower. Mom was walking with Gram. I was sitting behind the check-in desk manning the office, a pad of very blank paper under my pen. Beside it was a page of facts Leaky gave me a while ago, but they hadn't inspired any ideas. Hard to believe, but I was actually trying to get homework done on Saturday—then have Sunday free to go out to the drive-in. Not that I was expected to work yet. I just wanted to look around.

The phone rang.

"Oak Acres Court," I answered.

"FREAK!!!" Leaky had caught up with me.

"Sorry, he can't come to the phone. Care to leave a message?"

"I'll leave a message all right!" Leaky growled. "This English homework is because of *you*, Toddler! Creative writing? What is *that*? And who ever said I can write?"

"Not me."

"Very funny. So funny, you gotta write it *for* me."

"No way, man!" I fired back. "Look, Lee, even *you* can

write one measly page." Truthfully, I had my doubts, but this was no time for honesty.

"Just give me something you already wrote," he insisted. "You owe it to me."

"I don't owe you! Besides, my other stuff doesn't even fit the assignment." I racked my brain for something to say that would get him off my back. My gaze hit the page of facts he had cribbed from library books. But it was his comments in parentheses that gave me an idea.

"Lee, you can do this," I said calmly. "You know how you're all the time telling me crazy things?"

"So?"

"So, just write like you're talking to me."

"Write like I'm talking?" He thought about it. "How do I talk?"

"You don't know how you talk?"

"I never listened."

"That makes two of us," I said and hung up.

I looked at my blank paper again. I was having as much trouble as Leaky, even though Mrs. Hagerwood had made it simple. "Just write about yourself." Then she'd added a suggestion: "Maybe write about something that happened to you recently. Anything at all. A slice of your life." She wanted details and feelings. We were free to write it like a diary entry, a letter to a friend, a news article—whatever we wanted. It needed to be at least one page and it was due Monday.

She had been looking *straight* at me when she assigned this homework. It was obvious my story had given her the idea. Should I write about having one of my stories inter-cepted by a teacher? That was lame. And embarrassing. So, what could I write about? The real question was, what could I write—about myself—that *wouldn't* be embarrass-ing? Nothing!

Actually I'd given embarrassment a lot of thought. I could write about blushing. I once determined that the reason I blushed so much was from an excess of blood in my body. I needed a vampire to drain some off, or maybe leeches on my neck to suck out the blood before it got to my face.

That was precisely the kind of thinking that usually started me happily creating a story. Not this time. There was only one thing I kept going back to. One thing I kept seeing.

I don't even know when I started writing.

It isn't mine. It's a stray.
A pup beside the road in the middle of nowhere.
I pick it up. Yeah, stupid, I know.
It's a her.
I stand beside the road. Wonder what to do.
A truck is coming. Big truck. Very loud.
It gets closer. The pup panics. Bites me.
I let go. I just let go.
She leaps from my arms. The truck is right there.
She falls under the wheels. Truck keeps going.
She's crushed and twisted. But alive.
Somehow. Impossibly.
Alive.
And crying.
Yipping and yipping. How can she still be alive?
There's someone else. Across the road. Where'd he
come from?
A guy. Guy says—That dog needs killing.
I yell something. He goes away.
Just me and the pup. What should I do?
The pup keeps crying. A sharp sound. It drills
into my head. It's hard to think. I look around.
In the weeds an old cardboard box. Flattened
with tire tracks.
I slide it under. Gently. Gently. To lift her.
Her cry quickens.
Blood on the road. In her nose.
I cradle her on my arms. Step over the guardrail.

Slip on the grass. Skid down the embankment.
She slides up against my chest.
Her crying is so close. So loud.
My head is pounding.
There's nothing down here. Just rocks. Weeds.
Litter.
I kneel. Set her on the ground.
Find a big rock. Dig under it. Struggle to turn
it over.
It leaves a shallow hole.
I pull her closer. Feel a tiny lick on my wrist.
I'm crying. Shaking.
I never knew what crying really was.
Ease the pup off the cardboard. Into the hole.
Impossibly her crying gets louder. Mindless. Ceaseless.
I pick up the rock. Raise it high.
I think—Get it done the first time.
I think—Do it hard.
I bring the rock down.

The crying stops
like a radio unplugged
in the middle of a sad song.

11

Sunday meant beds, laundry, church, then Sunday dinner. By mid-afternoon I had the dishes done and could ride out to the drive-in.

Again I was struck by how shabby the place looked in daylight. The movie screen was actually a tall, wide, flat building. The side facing the road was painted with giant peeling letters that announced what was obvious. DRIVE-IN THEATRE. On the near end of that building was a door marked "Office." It faced the ticket booth, which sat like an island in the asphalt entryway, creating two lanes. Another driveway exited from the far end of the building.

I tried the office door. Locked. I rode around the saw-horses barricading the driveway and coasted into the movie parking area, where I stopped, straddled my bike, and took in the sudden expanse. The movie screen looked naked in the light of day, a patchwork of weathered ply-wood painted carelessly in various shades of white. Inclined parking rows radiated out from the screen, and between every two parking spaces were speaker poles, none of them standing quite straight. Huddled low and flat, in the middle of the lot, was a dingy concrete building—the snack bar. On the side facing the screen, two tiny dark projector windows seemed to squint in the sun. A candy bar wrapper, blown by a gentle breeze, tumbled toward me in greeting, catching in the spokes of my front wheel. I watched it struggle to get through.

"So, pick it up how 'bout it?"

I looked up. Rat had stepped out from behind the snack bar and stood watching me, a partially filled trash bag behind him.

I bent down and grabbed the wrapper.

"It's official," he said, grinning. "You're on the job!"

As I rode over to him, he opened his trash bag. I stopped a few feet away and tossed the wadded paper in like a free throw.

"Swish! Dog Man scores!" he said.

It was like being punched. I looked at him, trying to absorb what he had just called me. He pulled off his sunglasses and returned my gaze. He wore a T-shirt with rolled sleeves, jeans, work gloves, and boots. The bridge of his nose curved slightly—maybe broken once. A pale scar bisected one eyebrow. His mouth traced a thin, easy smile. I couldn't see anything in his expression that looked like ridicule or sarcasm. He just seemed watchful, content to simply wait for me. I decided to let the *Dog Man* comment go.

Instead I asked, "You serious? I mean, start work now?"

"Over there," he said, pointing at a grocery bag sitting in the shade of the snack bar.

I dropped my bike, went to the bag, and knelt to open it. Inside were two sweating cans of soda and a pair of gloves on a stack of folded trash bags.

I looked back at him. "Did you expect me today? Because I never said for sure I'd take the job."

"I figured, how could you *not* want to work here?" He spread his arms wide.

I shrugged, picked up the gloves. Under them I saw something I couldn't understand, it was so out of place. I dropped the gloves and picked up my transistor radio. Slowly I stood and turned to Rat, holding it out. "What . . . what's this?"

He watched me for a second before answering. "I found it. Battery's dead. You can have it."

"But this . . . is mine," I said.

Rat didn't reply.

"I left it. On the rocks."

"Yeah," said Rat. "That's where I found it."

"I left it playing, you know, so the pup . . ." I couldn't find the rest of the words.

"I guess I figured that," said Rat.

I looked up at him. "But you *took* it!"

"I *found* it," he repeated.

"Why . . . ?"

He shrugged. "I was just lookin' around. Yesterday. After we talked. Curious, you know. Wondered how your story ended. I went down by the river. Found your pile of rocks. Found that radio. It was still on, but the batteries were dead. It wasn't doing much good anymore. So . . ."

I studied the station numbers. Clicked it on and off a couple times. "There was a song."

"Yeah?"

"'Layla.'"

Rat waited.

"It came on . . . just before I saw the pup."

He tugged on the cuffs of his gloves.

"It all happened—the pup, the truck, all of it—happened during that one song. It was still going when I put the radio down on the rocks. How could that be? How could all that happen in one song?"

He said simply, "Long song."

———————————

Rat didn't talk much while we worked. Just stray wisecracks like, "How could someone dump a box of popcorn when there are starving children in China?" Or when he found a school textbook, he said, "Someone's in trouble now!" and dropped it into the trash bag. After my first impressions of Rat I wasn't a hundred percent sure why I had agreed to work with him. To get away from the motel, I guess. And for the free movies. But while picking trash side by side, we had fallen into a rhythm. After a few of Rat's goofy comments I relaxed a little.

It wasn't yet summer, but we were sweating when we dragged the last of the trash to the snack bar. Rat pulled off his gloves and sat in the shade. I joined him. He rummaged in the grocery bag and pulled out the two canned drinks. Tossed me one. It was warm. When I opened it, foam spewed all over my lap. In the middle of swigging his drink Rat laughed so suddenly, it sprayed out of his mouth.

"You shook mine up, didn't you!"

Rat kept laughing.

"Think it's funny?" I stood up, gave my can a quick shake, and blasted him. He returned fire. I dodged and he came after me. Our cans were quickly emptied. We were soaked, and grinning like idiots.

"Man, I got you good!"

"Yeah? Least I didn't wet my pants."

I looked down at my lap. Tried to wipe my face, but my shirt was drenched too.

"Come on," said Rat. "Let's get cleaned up." He pulled out keys and unlocked an "Employees Only" door at the back of the snack bar. I followed him into a dim, low-ceilinged kitchen, where we rinsed off and wrung out our shirts.

Back outside, I picked up my bike and radio. A breeze started drying my shirt immediately, and my arms glowed with the beginnings of a sunburn.

"That's all for now, Dog Man," Rat said. "If you want to come back in a couple hours, you can meet Mr. Huber. Or wait 'til you start next Friday."

Dog Man again. And again the name jarred me, though not as much. "What about those bags of trash?"

"I'll throw 'em in my mother's truck," he said, "when she gets back from town."

"So, what do you do until opening time tonight?" I asked, not ready to go home yet.

"Little as possible," he answered.

"Let me show you something."

He looked sideways at me.

"You have a bike, right?" I said. "Go get it."

12.

My shirt dried quickly as we biked along the highway heading away from town. We crested a rise, then rolled down a long gradual slope into open farmland. I led Rat toward the river, following a tractor road into the fields until we were surrounded by plowed rows.

"Here's the place," I said. "Make sure you walk between the rows." We left our bikes and walked, slow, silent, watching the ground to avoid stepping on the newly sprouted shoots.

Rat kept one eye on me, the other on his footing. After a few minutes, he asked, "So what are we looking at?" I didn't answer. Rat seemed content to wait, to just follow. A while later I was close to giving up when I finally spotted something, picked up my find, and handed it to Rat.

"A rock," he said dryly. "You really know how to have a good time."

"Look at it," I insisted. It was flat and smoothly rounded, like a large skipping stone except for two indentations on opposite edges. "That's an Indian fish-net weight. Those notches were for the net cord. It might be a thousand years old."

Rat handed it back. "If you say so."

I pocketed it and walked on. Some time later, I bent to the ground again. "Check! It! Out!"

"Dog Man scores!" Rat said. He carefully lifted from my hand a three-inch spear point.

"Keep it," I said. "I got bigger ones." Pleased that I now had his total attention, I couldn't stop myself from spouting off. "People think this valley's been inhabited for eight thousand years. Some of the flint these points are made of came all the way from the Michigan area."

Rat looked around his feet with new interest.

"Let's go back," I said. "Something else you gotta see."

Out on the highway again, I stopped and pointed into the field. "See where we were?"

"Yeah."

"See that very slight rise across the middle?"

Hand shading his eyes, Rat nodded uncertainly.

"Look close," I said. "From a tractor you wouldn't even notice it. It's so gradual from all the years of plowing. It's like a plateau just a little higher than the rest of the field. See it?"

"Yeah." Rat nodded. "Now I see it."

"Okay. Right along where the ground rises? That's where I find the most arrowheads and spear points. Must have been a village there."

Rat considered that. He looked west, then east, taking in the entire river valley. "No," he said.

"What?"

He stared into the field without answering.

"What do you mean?" I prodded.

"That wasn't the village. The village would've been closer to the river."

"How do you know?"

He shrugged. "That rise there? That's a fortification. That's where they fought."

We headed back toward town. At the top of the long hill, just before we got back to the drive-in, I pulled off the highway again. "One more thing." A dirt and gravel road angled down toward the river through rolling expanses of tall grass. About fifty yards in I stopped. "Let's wait here," I said, climbing off my bike. I sat in the dirt road facing west.

"Whatever you say." Rat sat beside me, the spear point in his hand. He rubbed it absently with his thumb. I had to admit—he knew how to wait. I was curious about his fortification comment. It made sense, but how would he know?

Before us, the field sloped down. A couple hundred yards away, a small round-topped hill rose again. The sun was in our eyes, lowering over the hill. The longer we sat, the louder the crickets chattered.

"Okay," I said. "It's starting."

I shaded my eyes with one hand and pointed toward the setting sun. Light raked down the east face of the hill. What had appeared to be an even growth of tall grass was suddenly dabbed with at least a dozen separate, soft oval shadows. "See those?"

"Sure do," said Rat.

"They're caused by very shallow indentations in the earth. Those are Indian grave sites. Maybe warriors, high on the mound like that. Only visible for a few seconds when the angle of light is just right."

Once, I showed this sight to Leaky. He flipped out. Thought it was so cool, he jumped up and ran to get to them. But it was farther than it looked, and there was a fence. He gave up. Now I watched Rat for some kind of reaction. With a hand shading his eyes, he stared in silence. Then without a move or a blink, his gaze just seemed to go long, like he was seeing all the way through the hill.

The sun continued to slide down the sky. Shadow quickly blanketed the entire grassy slope and it once again appeared perfectly smooth.

"Gone," I said under my breath, "like ghosts."

Rat didn't say anything. I watched a lone tree in the field. Its shadow doubled in length in just minutes as the sun continued to set.

"So, what's on your arm?" I asked to break the silence.

"Huh?" said Rat, almost like he was waking up.

"I thought I saw a tattoo when you had your shirt off. But it was kinda dark in the snack bar."

"Oh, that." He didn't elaborate.

I egged him on. "So, what? A girlfriend's name?"

No answer.

"Okay, I know. It says 'Mom.'"

"Nothin' like that."

I waited. When I finally decided he wasn't going to tell me, he did, sounding very far away. "It says, 'Firebase Ripcord, 506th Infantry.'" A few heartbeats later he added, "Vietnam."

My Dog
by Lee Simmons
English—June 12, 1972

So, like, I have a dog, you know. His name is Fuzz. He's
cool and all. But lately, he started this thing, see. He eats
cigarette butts. I have to walk him. That's my job, twice a
day. And he's all the time scarfing cigarette butts off the
sidewalk. It's bummin' me out because, you know, the whole
cancer thing. But he's fast. I jerk back on the leash, but
he's already munching away. My neighbor knows dogs. He said
I should put some hot pepper inside some butts. Put 'em out
on the sidewalk and let Fuzz suck up a couple. Maybe he'll
mellow out on the whole butt-eating thing. But Mom and
Dad don't smoke. And me, I'm too grossed out to go around
and, you know, pick up strangers' butts to put the pepper in.
So I just let Fuzz do his thing. Okay, so we're walking down
Seneca Street. And I go by Janet's house. Not by accident,
know what I mean? And there she is, out on her porch like
I hoped. Doing homework or something. I stop and wave.
And dig this. She comes out to see me. Well, mostly to pet
Fuzz. But that's cool. I am trippin'!!! Because she's standing
right next to me! So after I tell her Fuzz's name and his
breed and stuff, I'm outta things to say. She's pretty much
finished petting Fuzz. And she's about to go. So I'm thinkin'
it's say-anything time. I'm checking out her house and say,
"So where's your room?" She gives me a look like, "Weird!"
but then she points to a window. I coulda guessed because

it was full of stuffed bears. I say, "So you like teddy bears?"
She gives me another look like it's freaky I'm so interested.
Me, I'm needing something to say and I just start makin' up
stuff. I tell her I'm an artist, see, and what I'm good at is
stuffed animals, and I could do a group portrait of her teddy
bears all set up on her bed. I can tell Janet's wondering
what kind of wacko trip I'm on. But she's also stoked, right?
You know, thinking a drawing like that would be cool. Then we
both hear this sound, like, HURK, HURK, HURK. We look down
and Fuzz just pukes up all these cigarette butts on her shoe.
Oh, man! The butts are swimming around in this milky yellow,
stringy kind of gunk. And she goes, "E-e-e-e-o-ou!" and flicks
her foot. The stuff sprays all over Fuzz and on my pants.
She runs into her house. Then Fuzz goes and sniffs the stuff
he just hurled up. I lose it. I yank on the leash and we go
home. In a way, I guess it's okay that Janet's mad. Now I
don't have to do that teddy bear drawing. I mean, can you
imagine?

13

Monday. Mrs. Hagerwood asked for a volunteer to read their homework assignment aloud. Leaky's hand was the only one that went up.

"Okay, Lee. Go ahead."

He stood, grinned over at me, and began reading from a wrinkled sheaf of papers. "So, like, I have a dog, you know."

Mrs. Hagerwood interrupted, "Excuse me, Lee? Did I hear you right? 'So, like, I have a dog, you know'? Is that what you said?"

"Yes. I mean, that's how I wrote it," he explained, holding out his papers as if she could read them from across the room.

"Tell me about how you wrote it," she said.

"Well, you told us to write how we wanted. I wrote it, you know, like how I talk." He glanced at me again. I gave him a look that meant, *Don't you dare drag me into this.* He continued, "See, I talked into my dad's tape recorder. Like I was talking to a friend. Then I played it back and wrote it down."

"Okay." Mrs. Hagerwood nodded. "I like that. Go ahead."

By the time Leaky had finished, the entire class was hysterical. Even Mrs. Hagerwood was cracking up. Good thing Janet wasn't in our class. After that, no one else wanted to read. So Mrs. Hagerwood used the vilest trick of her trade. From a shelf by her desk she picked up the feared and loathed Volunteer Box.

A hush fell over the room. She pulled out a slip of paper with a name on it and announced, "Ann Carpenter." The rest of the class audibly exhaled in relief. Ann stood up, blushing.

It's not fair how some people look cuter when they blush.

Ann read about a trip to the dentist's office. I was spellbound. I pictured myself as her dentist, hovering over her mouth. I would make small talk. But I wouldn't expect her to answer me with tools crammed in her mouth. I would take everything out each time to let her speak. Her check-up would take longer that way, but other patients would just have to wait.

Coming out of my daydream, I realized Ann had finished and Mrs. Hagerwood was pulling another name out of the box.

"Todd, would you like to read next?"

I felt dizzy with panic. She had never said anything about reading our work aloud. I looked down at my English notebook. It was closed, but my written piece was sticking out the top. I could see the first line. "It isn't mine. It's a stray."

Suddenly I couldn't believe I had put those words on paper. What was I thinking?

"No," I said weakly.

"No?" Mrs. Hagerwood asked.

"Sorry," I said. "I didn't do the assignment."

For the rest of class I couldn't face Mrs. Hagerwood. I studied my desktop. Every detail. Someone had carved: "Jimi Hendrix for President." Last November I drew a two-fingered peace sign. Recently, someone had scraped off one finger and left only the middle one sticking up.

After a couple more stories, Mrs. Hagerwood collected them and started a discussion about their differences, styles, that kind of thing. I remember one of her comments. "No one mentioned an element I found interesting in Lee's piece. The force of nature. I'm fascinated by natural or random elements in a story that confront the characters and alter their fates. What force of nature altered Lee's fate? Anyone?"

"Dog barf," Brian suggested.

"I was thinking about the dog itself," Mrs. Hagerwood said patiently. "Fuzz was an unpredictable element in the story, a force of nature that changed everything."

Someone asked if people could be forces of nature. "I suppose so." She nodded thoughtfully. "Some kinds of characters, in certain situations."

Leaky's hand shot up. "Am I a force of nature?"

Mrs. Hagerwood rolled her eyes. Gave up trying to develop the discussion any further. "Yes, Lee. From Janet's point of view? Definitely!"

"Far out!" he said.

She spent the rest of the period introducing our next assignment. Then the bell rang. Over the clamor of kids leaving, Mrs. Hagerwood called, "Todd, a moment please?"

When we were alone she asked, "What happened?"

I shrugged. "Guess I forgot." She waited. "See, I started a new job and . . . I can turn it in tomorrow."

"No. It's too late for that." She seemed disappointed. I was shocked. I couldn't remember another teacher who had ever noticed me enough to be disappointed, or impressed, or anything else. "In that notebook last week," she said quietly, "I saw a real writer."

Students for her next class started coming in.

"Okay?" she said to dismiss me. I turned and fled the room.

In the hall, I passed Leaky at his locker. "Cool story," I said, trying to sound happy for him. It came out pathetic.

"Toddler!" He turned with a big grin. "I am Force-Of-Nature Man." He pulled his unbuttoned shirt open. In six-inch Magic Marker letters, he had just written on his T-shirt, "F-O-N."

———

I had given up trying to find the pup's owner. It was time to face the medicine. But even a rabies shot to the gut seemed like a fair price to get out of Bailey's class early. I rode my bike to the hospital's out-patient clinic. It had been a fight to convince Mom I could handle going by myself. The doctor had assured us that the shots weren't going to cripple me or anything. Besides, I reminded her,

Gram would have to come too because she couldn't be left alone—and car trips just added to her confusion. Mom finally relented.

A nurse checked my arm. Said I didn't need the bandage anymore. Then gave me the shot in the belly, which was bad. Soon after, it got worse. Like they had stuck me with a lead pipe and left the pipe in. So I headed straight home.

When I got there, Mom handed me an envelope. "I found this in the mailbox. For you?" It was drive-in theater stationery and addressed simply, "Dog Man." I snatched it from her, hoping she wouldn't ask about the name. She didn't. I went to the kitchen and made a jelly sandwich. Used the morning paper for a plate. In the drive-in envelope I found a "Coming Attractions" movie hand-out. On the back was written, "My turn to show *you* something." I smiled and put it in my shirt pocket.

Then I spotted a newspaper article headlined, "Man in River Murdered." The only new information was that the man had been beaten to death "with an instrument like a nightstick or a small wooden bat." His identity and time of death were still under investigation.

As I ate, I started wondering if Hagerwood might, for the next assignment, accept a murder mystery based on the guy in the river. I considered the usual suspects. Aliens. Communist spies. Drug-crazed hippies. Or maybe something more realistic. I tore out the news story and went to my room.

What could Rat want to show me?

The way my gut ached I didn't even consider riding out to the drive-in. Good thing. Later that afternoon it rained. I put the murder mystery aside for another time. In fact, I already had an idea for the next writing assignment. Hagerwood called them "how and why stories." Stories that explained things were some of the first ones ever told. Like the creation story in the Bible, she explained. She also read one of Rudyard Kipling's *Just So Stories* about how elephants got trunks. Our assignment was to write a story like that. Again, we could write in any style. Fiction or nonfiction. It was due on Thursday.

In the pool of light under my desk lamp, one hand holding my aching stomach, I slipped into the writing zone. Put down the entire assignment in one sitting.

How Lee Simmons Got His Nickname
by Todd Anthony
English—June 15, 1972

It started with a bad hot dog at the year-end school carnival two years ago. Food, music, the dunking pool, ring toss games—all of that. Us sixth graders had to take shifts helping in the booths. We were rewarded with free prizes. Lee signed up to work the grill, turning burgers and rolling hot dogs. Because for that job the reward was "all you can eat."

Lee scarfed countless hot dogs during his shift, the last shift of the day, but he had his eyes on one more wiener. During an earlier shift, the hot dog in question, cooked to a bronze perfection, had accidentally slipped into a shallow trough at the edge of the griddle where all the scrapings went. There it lurked for hours in the afternoon sun, not on the heat of the fire but in a warm pool of sludgy grease. As Lee slathered that last hot dog with mustard and ketchup he failed to notice its faintly green shimmer. That was Friday.

Saturday morning came and went. Some of us guys had gotten together but no one had seen Lee all day. Finally, late in the afternoon, Brian picked up the phone. Lee's mom answered. She said, "Lee's indisposed." We couldn't figure out what that meant. So we rode our bikes to his house. On the way, I spotted Lee's little sister playing with a friend.

"He can't come out," she yelled, as if to say "Nya-na-nah-na-nah-na." Normally, we ignored his sister's tiny, obnoxious existence, but this time we stopped. She was pleased to have our full attention, and mimicked her mother: "He's indisposed."

"We heard that much," said Brian. "So what's his problem?"

A look of evil joy lit her face. "He's got the number-twos." We were suitably grossed out, so she added, "Daddy's afraid he'll leave a trail on the carpet to the bathroom."

It was simply wrong to leave her with such a grin of triumph. I said, "Looks like some of it got on your head." She stuck her tongue out as we rode off. But from the corner of my eye I saw her hand go up to feel her hair.

Fifteen minutes later we were doing something our teachers would have found unbelievable. We were writing. Well, mostly I was writing. A "get well soon" kind of thing. We felt it would be nice to send Lee a few thoughtful, caring words.

"How do you spell Montezuma?" I asked.

"Use it in a sentence," Adam said. He had just been in the school spelling bee.

I read what I had so far. "Hope you get over the

squirts. Or whatever you call it. Brian calls it happy crap. We think it's also known as the galloping trots or Montezuma's Revenge."

"Oh, _that_ Montezuma," said Adam. "I have no idea."

A brainstorming session followed. We invented names for it. Juicy toots, sewer stew, things like that. I passed the page around for approval, then folded and glued it shut with chewing gum. On the outside, I wrote, "To Lee."

"We can do better than that!" Brian insisted. "How about 'To Barf Butt.'"

"If it's too gross," I cautioned, "his mom might get mad and not give it to him."

When we finally stood at Lee's doorstep and handed the note to his mom, it was addressed: "To Leaky Cheeks."

She looked at us. Her eyebrows and lips searched for the right expression. Her face twitched as if to say, "You think this is funny? You are disgusting! You're on the road to hell and you want to take my Lee with you." Finally, the parts of her face took a vote and her mouth announced the verdict. "He's upstairs. You may take this to him yourself."

We looked past her into the house. At the top of the darkened staircase, a light glowed from down the hallway where the bathroom was. Suddenly we heard the violent sound of suffering. BLABBIT-A-

BLIT-A-BLIT-A-BLIT! It resonated from deep within a water-filled porcelain bowl. Then we actually saw it coming. The Smell. It looked like the churning air over a hot highway. It oozed to the end of the hall and gathered like a wave. It spilled onto the staircase. The smell rippled and tumbled down the steps. At the bottom it pooled, convulsed, then rolled toward the open door. It struck Lee's mom full on the back, blowing her hair and skirt. Her eyes lost focus.

I thought, How could anyone survive that? Then the truth dawned on me. Lee's mom hadn't survived! It had killed her and taken control of her body. That explained her odd facial expressions. Now she was luring _us_ into that house of horrors, to turn us into the walking dead like her! She reached out and The Smell hit us.

Stumbling backwards off the porch to save ourselves, we all spoke at once. "No thanks!" "Just give it to him." "We got stuff to do." "Bye now."

And that's how Lee Simmons got his nickname, Leaky.

14

Tuesday after shot number two, I stopped at my river clearing to feel sorry for myself for a minute. Something was snagged on a branch in the shallows. Rain always pushed trash downriver, and last night's rain had come down hard. This particular piece of flotsam was a muddy green baseball-style cap with some kind of military insignia. I thought I'd show it to Rat since he had been in the army.

That was a piece of information I was still working on. Rat—a Vietnam vet? He didn't look much older than me. At the Indian mound, right after he mentioned Vietnam, he'd said he had to get back to work. I was left with millions of questions.

What was it like? Did you have to kill anyone? Were you scared? How old are you?

They were questions I had no idea how to ask. The hat would be a good way to at least bring up the subject. In my pack I kept a plastic rain poncho for bad weather. I wrapped the wet hat in it, went home, and lay on my bed holding my stomach. Rabies shots sucked. It rained again. All night.

On Wednesday morning I got Mom's okay to go out to the drive-in after the hospital. Told her Rat needed to see me. She looked at me quizzically. "About the drive-in job," I explained, though I didn't really know. And she had to be assured once again, "The rabies shots are no sweat!"

Yeah, right.

I don't know why I insisted on going to the clinic alone. I just felt better that way. Not that it felt *good,* don't get me wrong. Each shot was like a kick in the gut. But maybe I deserved it.

It rained all day, letting up just before last period. At the hospital, I got shot number three.

Eleven to go.

At the theater, Rat was unlocking the office door, carrying a cardboard box. "Get my message?"

"You wanted to show me something?"

"Come on in," he said. "Bring your bike."

I followed him. The office was a small, low-ceilinged room thickly painted school-bus yellow. A beat-up desk squatted beneath a heap of papers, clippings of movie ads, and half-full cups of scummed-over coffee. Rat dropped his box onto the mess, and a few movie flyers spilled out of the open top. Behind the desk, a hallway led back into darkness. The most memorable feature of the room was a wall of photographs beside the desk. Thirty or forty cheaply framed, eight-by-ten, black-and-white pictures hung ceiling to floor. All were of women from the 1940s or '50s posing in bathing suits.

Rat picked up a clipboard, then saw me gazing at the wall. "No, that's not what I wanted to show you," he said. "Those are Mr. Huber's."

"He's a photographer?"

"Was," Rat grunted. "He used to work in Florida. Some tourist department."

Surrounded by the pictures was a cluttered cork bulletin board. I noticed a Polaroid snapshot tacked there. It was of Rat and another guy by the snack bar, half-filled trash bags at their feet.

"Is that Mr. Huber?" Immediately I realized it couldn't be. This guy wasn't old enough to be taking pictures in the 1940s.

"No, but Huber snapped that picture." Rat tossed the clipboard onto the desk. "Leave your bike here. And your backpack."

I followed him outside. Rat crossed the theater entrance and headed down the side driveway, past his house. Around back, a rusting pickup truck was parked. I noticed an empty rifle rack in its back window. And someone inside that I couldn't make out. We came around behind it and I saw the passenger door hanging open. Rat never slowed his pace. The yard turned from weeds to brush to trees. I glanced back at the truck as we were about to enter the woods. A woman slouched in the passenger seat, staring ahead as if the truck was still going somewhere. She looked pale, dark around the eyes, with stringy hair. I've seen dead people before, at funeral homes. And except for her eyes being open, this woman looked like *them*. My foot snagged a fallen branch. I stumbled into the woods and lost sight of her.

Rat followed no trail that I could detect but moved quickly and I couldn't quite catch up. The river, I realized, was our destination. But I was amazed at how far we had to go before water showed through the trees. By then, Rat was far ahead. He stepped down through some tall weeds and disappeared behind a huge maple. The tree was crowded by several smaller but still sizeable trees. When I got to the water's edge Rat was gone.

"Up here, shortie." He was above me, on a small platform. Lengths of two-by-four were nailed up the tree trunk—steps that weren't visible from the direction we had come.

My sore stomach made it seem like a long climb. By the time I stepped out onto the little deck, Rat was gone again. More steps led to a much larger platform fifteen or sixteen feet higher. When my head emerged through an opening in that upper deck, Rat was stretched out like he'd been relaxing for hours.

"This is so amazing!" I whispered in awe.

"Yeah. Ain't it?" he said, grinning just like a kid.

15

Rat gave me a tour, if you could call it that. The deck was at least twelve feet square. Two wooden footlockers made a low wall along the back edge of the platform farthest from the river. Beside the entryway I had just climbed through was a stack of firewood. Overhead, three pieces of camouflaged tarp were stretched for rain cover.

The footlockers were army green, bolted to the deck and padlocked. In one he had a blanket, a wad of mosquito netting, a boat cushion, and nylon rope. "Can you believe I found most of this stuff along the river?" he said. "People come out and party. Then they stagger off and leave their junk behind." He had tools too, a can of nails, a small coffeepot, a motley assortment of cans—beans, ravioli, things like that—and a couple jugs of water. The other footlocker was filled with dry firewood, a blackened rectangle of wire grill, and a sealed jar of matches.

I turned and looked at what I really loved. The fire pit. Right in the middle of the deck was a hole. A large stainless steel sink hung down inside it, resting by its lip edges on a couple lengths of galvanized pipe. Rat explained that when the sink got hot, the pipes kept it from making direct contact with the wood deck.

"Check out the view." We sat on the river side of the platform, feet dangling high over the water. On the opposite shore were shale cliffs and dense woods. I looked up and down the river. No houses.

"You could live up here!"

Rat laughed. "Maybe. But mostly, if I want to get away for a while, here I am." He added dismissively, "I don't know. It's just something to do."

I knew exactly what he was talking about. It was his place to disappear. Like my own little clearing by the river. But spectacular! We were quiet for a while, the silence broken only by distant geese.

"Hey," he said, "I heard from a guy working in the snack bar that there's no school Friday. That right?"

"Yeah, some kind of teacher day."

"Can you start work Thursday night? Thursdays are slow. Be a good time to show you around."

"Sure. Maybe. I'll ask."

"Also, I could use your help Saturday morning. Not for trash duty. I want to get some wood. Build a low wall back there." He pointed behind the footlockers. "Maybe bring walls partway out on each side too. With a slant roof to cover, oh, maybe, out to the fire pit."

"Sounds cool," I said.

"Guy I know is building a house. He lets me go through his scrap pile. Last time, I got a lot of this wood in one pickup load. But carrying it down here to the river is a hell of a job." Regardless of it sounding like hard work, it felt good that he wanted—or needed—my help.

Mention of the pickup reminded me. "Hey, Rat, who was back there? In the truck?"

He kept staring out over the river. As he did, all the looseness of that tree-house-loving kid I glimpsed not ten minutes ago seemed to harden like a knot. Then he looked at me. "That's my mom."

He said it through a fake smile. Said it like on *Leave It to Beaver* or something. Like life was perfectly wonderful and Mom wasn't really sitting in a zombie stupor in a rusted truck parked in weeds behind the house.

"Is she . . . " I hesitated.

"Is she what?" There was a low, hard edge in his voice.

"Is she . . . you know . . . okay?"

He stared at me. The crazy smile drained away and he said, "No." Said it with certainty, like she would never be okay.

He didn't say anything more. After a long silence, I offered a couple items from my vast knowledge of the river—about the Civil War prison camp that once stood on the shore not far away, and the location of my best fishing hole. Eventually I realized I was talking to myself. I shut up.

Obviously I had crossed some unseen line by asking about his mom. Just when I thought I was getting to know him, and I was relaxing, there I was back to feeling unsure again. He gazed over the river, his eyes restless. They flicked here and there, searching the trees on the far shore.

I had never before met a guy like Rat. Never before had I tried hard to figure someone out. I had always diddy-bopped along, day to day, never going too deep. And never needing to. Suddenly, high above the river there, I had a thought, an observation—the kind of thing I never usually paid attention to. Suddenly I knew that what I was seeing in Rat's restless gaze was . . . fear.

A long time passed. I didn't know how to break the silence. I'm telling you, it can get strange sitting side by side with someone who's not saying anything. Not doing anything. So—and this sounds stupid, but anyway—I decided to try a Rat thing. You know, how he's so good at waiting.

So I sat quietly. And I waited.

10

I had every intention of volunteering to read my story. I figured I owed it to Mrs. Hagerwood. Maybe get back on her good side. And Leaky was going to love it!

I thumbed through my story for the millionth time, for anything I might want to fix at the last minute. For some reason, this time, my eye caught the part near the end, about Lee's mom being killed by the smell, becoming a zombie. And I thought of Rat's mom. I don't know exactly how to describe this, but something happened in me. No. More like something had *already* happened and I was only now realizing it. What I had written, what I had thought was so hilarious two days ago, now left me feeling . . . nothing. I remembered one of the notes Mrs. Hagerwood had jotted on my story last week: "A bit juvenile for my taste."

The secure zone of comfort I had always enjoyed while writing stories—and reading them to friends—vanished in a cold rush. The story in my hand, I realized, wasn't the kind of thing I wanted to write.

It got worse. Because while I was sitting dumbfounded

by the thoughts in my head, a half-dozen guys raised their hands to volunteer reading. Guys who *never* raised their hands. Even Mrs. Hagerwood was startled.

Apparently Leaky's dog-barf story had inspired the more reluctant writers in the room to explore a now vastly expanded range of acceptable subject matter. And they were all eager to share with the class. One at a time Mrs. Hagerwood called on them and we heard stories about snot and cat turds and slime.

Even Brian read one, a true story. I'd heard about it when it happened. About his little brother, Danny, back when he was new at sitting on the toilet. Danny's butt was so skinny, he worried about falling in. For extra support, Danny would put his hands on the seat rim beside each butt cheek, gripping inside the seat hole. That way, he was able to rest some of his weight on his knuckles while he did his business. But he was shy about it. One time he locked the bathroom door, climbed onto the seat, and perched on his knuckles. Somehow, Danny lost his grip. Both hands slipped off the seat and down into the hole. His butt immediately followed and wedged itself in, pinning his wrists against the seat. He was stuck. He couldn't move his arms, and kicking his feet just wedged him in deeper. When he felt cold toilet water with his fingertips, he screamed bloody murder. His parents came running, but the door was locked. They called him. Danny was screaming too much to answer. Fearing the worst, his dad bashed the door open with his shoulder and fell into the bathroom just inches from Danny, who screamed even louder. His mom pulled Danny out of the toilet like a cork out of a giant bottle. But my favorite part was Mrs. Hagerwood's question at the end: "Tell me, Brian. How does your story fit the assignment? I mean, what makes it a 'how or why' story?"

"Oh," Brian said, "I . . . uh . . . forgot to read the ending." He stared intently at his paper, frowning with concentration. Finally he said, "That's why Dad bought a new bathroom door."

Mrs. Hagerwood smiled knowingly. "Nice save!" she said. As soon as the next volunteer started reading, Brian pulled out his pen and added his improvised line.

Five guys in a row read one gross-out tale after another, and I sat in deepening misery. Not only did I feel disillusioned about my own story, but now I saw it as just one more gross-out. One among many. I felt sick. I knew I had to turn it in, but . . . I wanted to wad it up. I wanted to burn it. I wanted to never again have to write another story for Mrs. Hagerwood.

I wanted to just write what I wanted to write.

And I had no idea anymore what that was.

17

When I first talked to Mom and Dad about only working Fridays and Saturdays until school let out, I hadn't remembered—the upcoming Friday there was no school. So, with Mom's permission, I started that Thursday night.

The newspaper ad called it "An Evening with Alice!" The three movies were *Alice in Wonderland* followed by *Bob & Carol & Ted & Alice* followed by *Alice's Restaurant*. It was a bizarre mix of films obviously designed to bring out the hippies.

Rat had said Thursdays were usually slow. Plus, a drizzle of rain promised to make it even slower. When I got there Mr. Huber hadn't yet arrived. "Always late," Rat said. With an hour until showtime he took me out back to introduce everyone.

A short woman named Jackie ran the snack bar. She had one glass eye and multicolored teeth. Two guys working with her were introduced as her sons, though they had different last names. Behind her, popcorn erupted and cascaded from the kettle. Jackie held two boxes under the spill, then handed the boxes to us. "It don't git any

fresher'n 'at!" she said. She was right. It was the best popcorn I'd ever eaten.

Rat knocked on a door across from the snack counter.
The projection room. A scowling, middle-aged guy looked
out. Oiled-back hair and a pencil mustache. Rat introduced him as Bill, who said to me, "See this room?" He
thumbed back over his shoulder. "It's union only. Means
show me your card or stay out, got it?" The door shut.

Rat shrugged. "Bill must like you. He doesn't usually
talk that much."

We ate our popcorn, waiting for a letup in the rain that
was now pouring. No luck. Finally we jogged back to the
front, getting soaked. I followed Rat into the office. "There
are paper towels in the bathroom," he said, pointing down
the hallway behind the desk. I dried off and brought some
out for Rat.

"Cup of coffee?" he asked.

No one had ever just outright offered me coffee before.
"Got a Coke?"

"Back at the snack bar. Through the rain."

"Okay, coffee then. I guess."

I followed him back down the hall. Just beyond the
bathroom door where the hallway ended, so did the ceiling. I stepped into the back room and gaped up into the
dim interior heights of the screen building. The space
overhead was a crisscrossed maze of wood beams and
diagonal braces. The wall to my left, the movie screen
side, went straight up. The wall to my right, the highway
side, leaned gradually in, making the roof no more than

four feet wide but fifty or sixty feet long. Amid the muffled patter of rain, I heard a faint flutter of wings high up in the darkness.

Rat switched on a light. "Cream, sugar?"

"Sure."

He stood at a table with an electric coffeepot and all the fixings. The single light over the coffee also lit a grid of wooden boxes. There, stacks of red and black plastic marquee letters were shelved alphabetically. Farther back in the gloom, I could make out lawn mowers, tools, boxes of junk, and a back door.

Rat handed me a paper cup of coffee. I tried a sip. It was too hot to taste at first, scalding my tongue. When I finally got a mouthful down, I nearly gagged. I don't know what drinking from an ash tray of cigarette butts would taste like, but this had to be close.

"More sugar?" Rat asked.

"A lot more!"

We took our coffee outside to the ticket booth. The rain had nearly stopped by the time Mr. Huber finally arrived. He wasn't what I thought a bathing beauty photographer would look like. He was short, round, bald. Wheezed when he breathed. And his breath—oh man! Like something had crawled in his mouth and died! He squeezed beside me in the tiny box office booth to demonstrate the ticket dispensing machine. When he breathed on me, I nearly puked up my popcorn. Outside, Rat watched through the box office window, grinning at my misery.

It was such a slow night, Mr. Huber thankfully retreated

to the office. Cars began trickling in. Rat took the money—adults, a dollar; twelve and under, fifty cents—and passed the cash in through the window slot. I punched up tickets and made change. Along with ticket stubs, Rat handed each driver a flyer advertising next week's movies.

He relaxed into a running commentary about the cars and customers. After a junker chugged inside, Rat said, "Be lucky if we don't have to tow him outta here tonight." A red Mustang convertible went through with kids on a double date. A pretty girl was driving. Watching them disappear inside, Rat said, "Whoo-ie! Good thing *I'm* out here, 'cause you're too young to look in *her* lap!"

Later, a big, low-slung car drove up with just a guy and a girl. They paid and Rat watched them go by. For the moment, there were no other cars in line. Rat looked at me. "That car there? Trunk's nearly dragging on the ground."

He stepped into the ticket booth and pushed a speaker button. "Mr. Huber, I need some help for a minute, please."

"I'm on my way," came the reply.

"What's happening?" I asked.

"Come on. Let's have some fun."

As Mr. Huber came out of the office, Rat and I were already jogging back into the theater. It was dark now, barely raining, and the movie had started. The low-slung car was several rows beyond the snack bar, pulling up to a speaker. When we got there, the driver was at the back of the car, opening the trunk. Two more guys and two girls climbed out, all of them talking low, giggling, and popping cans of beer.

I stopped short. It looked like trouble. But Rat stepped in among them and gazed into the now empty trunk. "That *had* to be a tight fit," he said with mock admiration. The group around him fell silent. Rat added, "That'll be four more dollars, please."

I was holding my breath, thinking, *Rat's crazy!* The guys were all bigger than him. After a moment of tense silence one guy asked, "What gave us away?" A buddy answered, "He heard you fart!" They laughed and reached for their wallets.

Back at the ticket booth, Rat handed Mr. Huber the money and briefly described the scene at the car.

Mr. Huber said, "After a job like that, I bet you two could use a pizza." He added grandly, "On the house!"

"It's always on the house," Rat deadpanned.

"Well, tonight you finally earned it."

We all laughed. Rat sent me back to get it.

13

Friday, my day off from school, it rained all morning. I made beds and painted the laundry room. After lunch I sat at my desk and tried to write something, anything. But nothing came. That afternoon I rode my bike to the hospital. Shot number five.

Returning home, as I rode up to the office I saw a folded note taped to the door. Mom had scrawled on it, "TODD!" I pulled it off. Inside, she had hastily written, "Gram wandered away. I'm searching. Stay here in case she comes back."

This hadn't happened before, but maybe we had just been lucky. Gram was feeble in the head, but she could still walk. I dropped my bike and looked around. Mom's car was still in the parking lot. She must have been searching on foot. Suddenly I had an image of Gram walking out onto the highway.

And a cement truck slammed into my mind.

I took a couple unconscious steps toward the road. But stopped. Mom wanted me here. I turned, looked at Gram's cabin. What could I do? How could I just wait? Then it hit me. I hadn't read to Gram all week. Hadn't sat with her.

Hadn't walked with her. Hadn't even thought about her.

How could I have forgotten her like that?

I couldn't stand still. I paced across the driveway, walked back along the cabins, pointlessly looking around corners where Mom was sure to have already checked. The motel seemed deserted. The only other car besides Mom's was a pale green junker parked at the end room. Some guy was still there from the night before. I hadn't changed his bed because only Mom or Dad dealt with rooms that were still occupied.

I hoped Mom would get back soon. Cars were sure to start pulling in for the night. Friday nights could get busy. And I had to be at the drive-in soon.

Geez! Thinking only about myself again. I meant to say I hoped Mom would get back soon—*with Gram.*

That's how easily I had forgotten her for a week. But so much was happening lately. Starting with that pup. The rabies thing. Rat. The drive-in. Even the writing assignments. Everything was crowding my mind.

I realized I wouldn't be able to hear the office phone from way out here. Mom might call. Just as I turned to go back, the old junker car creaked. Very slightly. All by itself. I couldn't see anyone inside. Then something moved in the backseat, a shadow within a shadow. I stepped closer and peered in through a grimy window. Gram was nestled down against the far back door, asleep, but shifting her position.

"Gram!" I yelled, and grabbed the rear door handle nearest me. It was unlocked and the door opened with a rusty metallic screech. I bent in and touched her shoulder gently. "Gram?"

She opened her eyes and looked around, confused. She struggled into a sitting position and smiled hopefully at me. "Are we there yet?"

The backseat was tattered and sunken. The car was a pigsty and probably stunk before Gram had climbed in, but I could tell she must have gone to the bathroom.

"Yes, we're here," I said. I reached in to take her hand.

"What the hell?" a voice boomed.

It startled me and I straightened. A heavily built guy stood in the doorway of the end cabin. He was unshaven, with a dirty T-shirt, pants wrinkled like he had slept in them.

"What're you doin' you little son of a . . . ?" Then he saw Gram in the backseat. His face twisted with disgust and rage. "What in hell's going on?"

"I'm sorry," I said. "My grandmother got in your car by mistake. She's not right in the head. She just—"

"Get away from my car!" he bellowed and took a step outside. He staggered a little, drunk or stoned or something. I felt fear and anger flood through me.

"Look. I said I'm sorr—"

"You heard me! Get your ass outta here!" He took a couple menacing steps toward us. "NOW!" he roared, clenching a fist.

I reached back into the car, grabbed Gram by her armpits, and dragged her out. I was startled by how little she weighed.

"Oo-o-w," Gram protested weakly.

There was a wet spot on the seat where she had lain. With my arms under hers, in a bear hug from behind, I clumsily hauled her away from the car and kicked the door shut. The guy glared at me until I began pulling Gram toward the office, dragging her heels over the asphalt. He went back in his room and slammed the door.

I stopped and stood Gram up on her feet. She was shaken, off balance from my rough handling. And I wasn't exactly feeling mellow myself. I held her shoulders and worked my way around to her front. Made eye contact.

"Are you all right, Gram?" I asked.

She tried to speak but what came out were prayer-like whispers. Her quivering hands fussed with the buttons on my shirt.

"Let's go home now. Okay?" I positioned myself at her side, one arm around her back and one supporting her elbow. "Can you walk now?" I asked.

I carefully nudged her forward. Gram took a half-step, frowned, then stopped. She pursed her lips as if to say, *Ooh,* and looked up, stricken with shame as she realized she had wet herself. Her head dipped, then she looked back up at me with an uncertain smile. Said timidly, "I don't believe we've met."

The motel never seemed so huge to me, helping Gram, with her tiny unwilling steps, all the way back to her cabin. We were just nearing her door when Mom, wide-eyed and frantic, jogged in from the highway. She saw us, stopped, and gasped, "Oh-dear-God-in-heaven!" And she burst into tears.

19

I sat outside while Mom bathed, dressed, and settled Gram on the couch. Gram was fine. *She* no longer knew what had happened.

Mom joined me. She kept explaining and blaming herself for leaving Gram alone in a lawn chair. She thought she could make a quick run to the laundry room. Get one load out and start another. We have an extension phone there and a call came in, which she answered. When she finally came back out, Gram was gone.

Like me, her first thought was to check the highway. "Then I ran around all the cabins. Twice! Must have looked like a crazy woman. I saw that car. It never entered my mind she would actually get in that filthy thing! By then so much time had passed. I wrote you the note. I ran to the gas station, then back toward town, knocking on doors. Hoped maybe someone found her, took her in. I must have just missed seeing you come home."

I still felt rattled by the guy. He had scared me, sure. I'd never before been on the receiving end of such unthinking hostility. But I was angry too. More like *hate*. Mom always taught me not to even use the word *hate*. As if it was profanity. But the feeling had detonated inside me. One minute I didn't know this guy existed. Next minute I hated him!

I didn't say all that to Mom, but described what the guy had said. She was so shook up, I wasn't sure she was listening.

Finally, from the phone in Gram's room Mom called Dad. Began telling him what happened. I didn't want to hear it again. I crossed the driveway and got a drink from the machine. Sitting on the curb I stared out at the road without seeing the traffic. It started raining again. I just sat there anyway.

Mom came to Gram's screen door, hugging her elbows. "Your father's coming home from work." She stood there a few more seconds, then went back inside.

I was astonished. To my knowledge, Dad had never done that before—left work early. What had Mom said that would make him come home? I mean, the actual emergency was over. Maybe it was just that she sounded exhausted.

All at once I knew why he was coming. Because I was leaving Mom alone and going to work at the drive-in. He was going to be mad! He hadn't wanted me to take that job in the first place. The drink machine made plenty of money for me, right?

Yeah, right!

He got home faster than I would have thought possible. His car skidded to a stop on the wet pavement in front of

Cabin 1. He didn't seem to notice me as he rushed into Gram's room. I crossed the driveway and stepped up to the screen door. Gram was on the couch. Dad and Mom were standing in each other's arms, Mom crying, Dad whispering in her ear.

From outside the screen door I heard Mom describe all that happened. She *had* listened to my part of the story. When she finished, Dad headed for the door.

"Honey . . . ?" she started.

"I'll be right back." The screen door slapped shut behind him. He glanced my way and said, "Stay here."

I stayed. For about five seconds. Then I followed him, slowly, not trying to catch up. He walked straight to the end cabin and pounded on the door. I stopped several cabins back, shocked. I had never seen Dad so angry.

The door opened a few inches. I couldn't hear words but could tell Dad was talking sharply. He pointed to the junker car, then toward Gram's cabin. The door opened wider and the guy said something back. Dad got louder. The drunk guy got louder too. They went back and forth like that, then Dad shouted so loud, I could understand his words. "I want you gone. NOW!"

The guy tried to slam the door in Dad's face. Dad stepped forward, caught the door, then abruptly shot it back inward. It smacked against the guy. Dad stepped into the room. Almost immediately, the drunk came stumbling out like he had been pushed. He fell against the hood of his car. Then his stuff came flying out the door. Loose clothes, a greasy brown duffel bag, a half-empty booze bottle. It littered the patch of grass in front of the car. Dad appeared in the doorway and pulled out his wallet. Threw down a wad of bills, a refund, I guessed. The guy tossed his stuff into the car. He growled a few final words that I couldn't make out, climbed behind the wheel, slammed the door, and cranked the engine.

I stepped out of sight beside the cabin where I had been watching. The green junker lurched back, then sprang forward, careening past my hiding place. Before reaching the highway, it abruptly swerved left. The driver's-side front wheel jounced up onto the sidewalk alongside the office. The rear wheel followed. The car's chassis scraped the curb, throwing off sparks. Just before it would have hit the office wall, the car lurched away, momentarily parallel to the building. A split second later it plowed into my drink machine. The machine gave with the impact and its entire front ripped away. Coins and broken glass flew out like confetti. The front tumbled forward, clattering between the moving car and the wall until it hit the glass office door, which shattered. The twisted metal slammed to a stop against the doorjamb, then fell into our front room. The car never slowed. It thumped down off the curb and fishtailed onto the rain-washed highway. As the guy picked up speed heading into town, I glimpsed his arm sticking out the driver's window, middle finger poking skyward.

When I got to the drink machine, broken bottles in their racks were still dripping onto the glass-strewn sidewalk. The bulk of the machine had partially rotated away from the wall and leaned out as if bending to see its own spilled guts.

Mom looked on from Gram's doorway. Dad came up behind me and put a hand on my shoulder. We stared at the wreckage. Spilled soft drink streamed around my shoes and mixed with the rain. Dad stepped forward and with the toe of one shoe, he pushed back some big shards of glass, revealing a spill of dimes swimming in cola. He smiled weakly and said, "Good thing you have that backup job."

I called the drive-in. Told Rat we had an emergency at the motel and I wasn't able to work that night. "I'm really sorry," I said, desperate for him to understand. "It's just that . . ."

A police car drowned me out as it pulled up to the office, its siren cutting off only when it came to a full stop.

Rat must have heard, because he said with a short laugh, "You have an emergency all right. Do what you gotta do. With all this weather, business is dead in the water anyway." Then he added, "Think you can still help me in the morning?"

"Oh, yeah," I said, remembering we were getting a load of wood for the tree house.

"Good. I'll pick you up at ten." He paused for a second. Then, "You okay?"

Just his asking made me feel better. "Sure," I said.

"All right. Don't worry about tonight. I got it covered."

20

Saturday morning, with beds made and chores done, I was inside reading *Huckleberry Finn* to Gram when Rat drove up. I latched her screen door from the outside with a newly installed hook. Mom and Dad both knew I was heading out to help Rat.

I climbed into the passenger seat. Rat was looking at the drink machine wreckage. I thought my "Out of Order" sign hanging on it was a nice touch, if I must say so myself.

"Part of your emergency?" he asked.

I shrugged. "Doesn't look like much now, I guess."

"Enough for the police to come," he observed.

Just then Mom rounded the corner with an armload of folded towels. Not entirely by accident, I'm sure. She likes to meet the people I hang out with.

"That your mom?" Rat asked, reaching for the door handle.

"Yeah," I said. We both got out.

Rat came around the front of the truck brushing his jeans as if they were dusty. "Pleasure to meet you, Mrs. Anthony."

"Nice to finally meet you, Mr. . . ." She hesitated just for a fraction, then finished, "Mr. Rat?" She laughed.

Rat didn't offer a real name, if that was what she was hoping for. He just nodded and shook her hand. Mom said something about taking care of her boy. Rat said, "Yes ma'am," sounding stiff, like he was respectfully taking military orders. We returned to the truck and pulled out onto the highway.

"So tell me about last night," he said.

While he drove I told my story in detail, like I was writing it as I spoke. There was a seriousness about Rat's listening that encouraged me. He shook his head at my description of the drunk guy, he groaned about the drink machine. I told how two policemen came out and took down our story. Dad showed them the guy's room registration card, including his license plate number. One cop sketched a small diagram of the motel layout and the movements of the car. It seemed as if they were treating the whole thing like a traffic accident. Maybe according to the law, that's all it was. I don't know. It felt like more than that.

Dad had asked, "You need to see his room?"

"Anything missing? Damaged?"

"No, I don't think so."

"Well, then, I think we're done here."

We started cleaning up. I gathered all the coins I could find. The glass office door wasn't a big problem. We had an inner wooden door. So we were secure.

As I talked I wasn't paying attention to where Rat was going, only that he'd made several turns and we were out in the country. I was about to describe cleaning the drunk guy's room, and what I'd found there, when we pulled off the paved road at a flower-shaped sign: "Welcome to Sweetwater." Realizing we were at our destination, I didn't continue. We bumped over a dirt road into a clearing. A handful of pickup trucks were parked in front of a large two-story wood building still under construction. Rat had said we were getting scrap wood from a guy who was building a house. But this was more like a barn on poles with a porch stuck to it. Windows were plentiful and scattered randomly, no two alike. A couple were intricate, freeform designs.

Rat parked near a pile of scrap lumber. Several long-haired guys were gathered between two trucks stacked with bales of insulation. A black guy with a major Afro and a tool belt waved to Rat and walked over crookedly, one leg stiff.

"Rat, my man!" he yelled. "Wuzz happenin'?"

"Not much, Flipper. What's up?" They slapped a chest-high, thumb-grabbing handshake.

"Jus' cool breezin', you dig?" They threw each other's hands away. "So, you hear about the naked hippie?"

Rat grinned. "No. Tell me."

"Naked hippie walks into a bar. Dude ain't wearin' nothin' but one shoe. Bartender, he at a loss for words. Jus' makin' conversation he say, 'Looks like you lost a shoe.'

"Naked hippie, he smile an' say, 'No, man. I *FOUND* one!'" The guy called Flipper laughed all out of proportion to the joke.

Rat chuckled and said, "I think I know that hippie."

"You and me both," said Flipper. "He buildin' this crazy house!"

"Is he here?"

He tilted his head toward the house. "Yeah, Bobby inside. So where that slack-jawed uncle of yours? We ain't seen him lately."

Rat shrugged, his smile vanishing. He looked at me. "I'll be right back."

Flipper watched Rat go, then looked my way. "So what's goin' down with you, Little Rat?"

I smiled at the name. "I work with him at the drive-in."

He snorted, "Ain't no one work with Rat. He work alone. Now, Rat there, he definitely one strange mother f . . ." He stopped himself. Looked at me. "Sorry, man. Looka me talkin' 'bout your boss man like that. Hell, maybe he your friend. My mama always say I be one rude and crude individual."

"And proud of it!" I added without thinking, employing one of Dad's habitual expressions.

I had said it in the spirit of his apparent good humor, but immediately feared he might take offense. Flipper's eyes opened wide. He was grinning. "Son! How you know all that?" He held his hand out. I took it and we shook the same way he and Rat had, like brothers, Flipper saying, "That's cool, that's cool." Then he threw my hand away.

"Call me Flipper on account of my foot here. Got my leg messed up bad by some damn Viet Cong booby trap. Check it out." At first I thought he was going to show me

some gross battle scars. Instead, he pulled a pack of cigarettes from his shirt pocket, laid them on the toe of one
shoe, and straightened. "You watchin'?" he asked. Lifting
his foot a half inch off the ground, he made an odd little
rotation of his hip. The toe of his shoe quivered and suddenly his foot twitched upward mechanically. The pack
of cigarettes popped a couple inches into the air, flipped
once, and landed back on his shoe.

Flipper grinned at me. "It be a wonderment how famous
I am 'cuza that. Almos' make it worth it."

I laughed and he seemed so pleased, I nearly asked him
to do it again. But I caught myself. It wasn't funny. He
didn't have scars to show because he didn't have a leg. It
was prosthetic. He must have seen my discomfort because
he added dismissively, "Don't mean nothin', man." He
picked up his cigarettes.

I said, "I'm Todd."

"That's cool. So, Todd, man, you hear 'bout the skeleton? He walk into a bar. Asks the bartender for a beer.
An' a mop."

I thought for a second that the joke would continue. Then
I got it. When I laughed, he laughed too, pointing at me and
crowing, "Hoo-ee! That one jus' sneak up on you! Fetch me
a beer an' a mop!" He cracked himself up all over again.

"So what you thinka this commune we buildin'?"

"Cool," I said. But I wasn't all that interested. Instead I
asked, "You know Rat very well?"

He thought about it. "Not much. Nobody know him
much."

"You asked about his uncle," I prodded. I remembered Rat saying how the pup needed killing and too bad his uncle wasn't around because he would have loved to do the job.

"You mean Unk? Yeah, I say that justa make Rat crazy. He hate that guy."

"Hates his uncle?"

"Oh, Unk ain't like no real uncle. See, when he a boy, Rat's mama tell him this guy his uncle, that guy his uncle. Now Rat call all his mama's boyfriends Unk. He tell me he can't even count how many uncles he have."

"Unk was part of your commune?"

"Mostly that dude jus' hang out. Smoke our dope. Do a little work. But he bring Rat along sometimes. That's how I know Rat. When we hear Rat call the dude Unk, we all call him Unk."

"Why does Rat hang out with him if he hates him?"

"Didn't hate him 'til he got to know him. See, Rat only been back in the world a little while."

"Back in the world?"

Flipper looked at me as if to say, *Don't you know nothing?* Patiently, he explained, "When you in Vietnam, ever-where else is 'the world.' So Rat, he git back from the jungle an' catch up to his mama. Meet his newest uncle. In no time at all, he hate the guy. But, like, he's stuck with him, 'cause the guy's an uncle an' all, you dig?"

We both got lost in our own thoughts for a few minutes.

"Anyhow," Flipper said, picking up a loose thread of

conversation, "Unk ain't been aroun' lately. You say you work at the drive-in? Unk do too, even though he be pretty worthless. You seen him?"

"No," I said. "Never met him." And I wondered. Because I thought I had met everyone who worked there.

21

Finally, Rat finished whatever socializing was apparently required before he could, in good conscience, raid the scrap pile. Flipper helped us toss a nice load of wood into the truck bed, complaining with a grin about spending his break time working for Rat. They shook hands again and we left.

Rat dropped me at home for lunch. I planned to bike out to the drive-in later. Help carry the wood down to the river.

Saturday's lunch—and the weekly family meeting—was quiet. Gram sat with us for a change and Dad actually helped with her food. Something unspoken was in the air. Dad seemed tired. I guessed they'd had their big talk again, last night or earlier today, about how to deal with Gram. Judging by Dad's look of defeat, I wondered if maybe they'd agreed on a nursing home.

I focused on getting through the meal unnoticed. No such luck. Dad suddenly looked at me as if I had just come to the table. "So, Rat work you hard this morning?"

I nodded. Mom and Dad thought I had been working

out at the drive-in, because . . . well, I never said any different. They probably wouldn't like where Rat had taken me. "Hey, Dad," I said, changing the subject. "A skeleton walked into a bar. Asked the bartender for a beer. And a mop."

Dad got it right away. I felt good about that. Gram watched Dad laugh and she grinned too. "I thought you'd like it," she said, and put her fork into her glass of milk.

The momentary happiness in Dad's face drained away. He reached across and took her hand gently.

"We're not done," I added as I helped Mom clear the dishes. "I need to go out again. Finish what we started this morning. Okay if I just stay until work time tonight? I can eat at the snack bar. Rat'll bring me and my bike home in the truck by eleven, same as before." Eleven wasn't closing time, but it was my curfew.

"All right," Dad said, "as long as your homework is under control." That was his auto-pilot answer, the kind I liked best.

"No problem," I said, heading for my room.

No problem? That wasn't entirely true. I still had no clue what to write for our next English assignment.

I wondered what kind of grade my Leaky story would get. The amazing thing was that Hagerwood hadn't seemed bothered by the gross-out stories. She discussed all of them seriously. "I don't care what you write about," she told us, "as long as you care enough to find the right words and the right way to tell it." But when she gave the next assignment I had to wonder if, despite being tolerant of our story topics, she wanted to avoid another batch of gross-outs.

"Historical fiction," she announced. "Write yourself into a true historical event that interests you. Write as if you're either a witness or a participant. This may require research"—a groan from the class—"so I'll give you a week. I want at least two pages this time."

She asked the class for examples of historical events they might write about. The ideas started out boring, like Columbus discovering America. When someone suggested the assassination of President Kennedy, violent themes entered the dialogue. All the gross-out authors suddenly got interested. Guys suggested things like the ambush of the gangster John Dillinger, and Wyatt Earp's shoot-out at the O.K. Corral. When Leaky mentioned chopping off heads during the French Revolution everyone started talking at once. In the eyes of many, creative writing was definitely getting cooler.

I grabbed my backpack. Threw a few things in: transistor radio, pair of gloves from Dad's workroom. What else? Cookies would come in handy. I looked at the spiral notebook folded open on my desk, the blank page glaring up at me. I thought back to last night, after the police, after the clean-up. I had sat in front of that blank page and stared out the window trying to think of an interesting historical event. But my brain was too churned up by Gram and the drunk guy and the drink machine. A school writing assignment just didn't seem real enough to care about.

I picked up the notebook, still folded open, and stuffed it into my pack. I pulled it back out. I hated that blank page. I was starting to fear it. Writing had never scared me before. I loved writing. A blank sheet of paper had always been a playground. Now it seemed more like a wall and I couldn't find a way in.

Just write something! I thought, *so it won't be blank.*

I picked up a pencil and scrawled across the top of the page: "Something."

Oh, cute!

I erased it. Wrote: "A skeleton walks into a bar."

Not exactly historical fiction, dimwit!

I erased it. Then I remembered Flipper's odd expression. I wrote: "Back in the world."

Strange sounding. But interesting. Back from where?

I erased it. The paper was smudgy where I kept erasing. I ripped it out and wrote on a clean page: "Vietnam."

Was that history yet? Some of it, I guess. The early part.

Rat's part.

I wondered if I could write about Rat.

Tell me about Vietnam, Rat. What was it like?

Under "Vietnam" I printed bold, like a title: "RAT."

What was life like in Vietnam, Rat? What was life like . . . for you?

I erased "Vietnam." Beside "RAT" I wrote, "LIFE." Said it aloud. "Rat Life."

At least it was something. It was a start.

I went to the kitchen and filled a small bag with cookies. Not ever wanting to forget Gram again, I went across to

Cabin 1. Gave her a cookie. She put it in her purse. I told her my plans for the day, not that she would remember. It was just something to say. She smiled up from the couch and said sweetly, "Give Todd my love."

"Sure, Gram," I said, then left, wondering how her mind could remember my name but forget who I was.

22.

I rode out to the drive-in. Started down the driveway to
Rat's house but stopped. Rat's mother had just stepped
off the porch. She walked—no, staggered—to the truck
parked by the house. It was empty of wood. She climbed in
and cranked the engine. Wanting nothing to do with Rat's
weird mom, I had retreated to the office door by the time
the truck climbed up the driveway and headed toward
town.

I knocked on the door. Nothing. Rode into the theater
parking lot. Rat was picking up trash. Like before, he had
extra bags by the snack bar.

"Dog Man!" he said, holding a couple limp french
fries. "Don't people know there are starving hippies in
Elmore!"

We worked side by side. Rat kept glancing at the sky. It
looked like the rain was coming back.

"Check it out!" He picked up a cigar butt, impersonated
Groucho Marx, then dropped it into the trash bag.

I joined the game when I found a half-eaten slice of
pizza. "Look! Lunch!" I gave Rat my profile, head back,

and faked like I was putting the whole slice down my throat.

He grinned. "Save some for me!" So I threw it at him.

We weren't quite done when it started raining. Rat kept working. But I was planning to be there until opening time—with no change of clothes. I ran to the snack bar, where I'd left my bike and pack. Pulled out the plastic rain poncho I always carried. When I shook it open, a ball cap fell out—the one that had washed up from the river. I'd forgotten about it. I pulled on the poncho and picked up the hat.

"Hey, Rat. I found something."

"Yeah?" But before I even got to where Rat stood, he reacted to what he saw in my hands. His voice went flat, playfulness gone. "Put it in the trash."

I stopped in my tracks. "No . . . I, uh, I didn't find this here. It washed up from the river. A few days ago."

Rat turned away and continued picking up trash. I barely heard him say, "Then it's yours."

"I was . . . just wondering . . ." I looked at the hat, groping for words. Rat was moving away, dragging his trash bag. Once again, out of the blue, he had gotten all weird on me. Seemed like I was always saying some innocent thing, like mentioning his mom, or his tattoo, and WHAM, he'd get weird. I was beginning to always feel afraid of saying some wrong thing.

"It looks military," I persisted. No response. "Thought . . . you might have lost it while working on your tree house. Dropped it in the water, maybe. I found it downriver."

Rat kept walking, his back to me. I thought about the assignment in my backpack. *Rat Life.* How could I ever interview him about Vietnam when he wouldn't even answer me about a crummy military hat? I decided if he wouldn't talk, I had to.

"It was wet when I found it. After a week in my backpack, man, it stinks! Hey, I wonder if Flipper would know something about it. He was in the army, wasn't he? I was thinking"—and this idea came to me even as I was speaking— "what if this hat belonged to that dead guy they found in the river? Wouldn't it be cool if this was . . ."

Rat, bent over a piece of trash, froze.

". . . some kind of evidence?" I finished.

He straightened, turned, and stared at me, rain streaming down his face. The day had darkened so much that, from where I stood, I couldn't see his eyes.

23

Rat's dark stare shut me up. The word *evidence* hung in the air. A trickle of rain found its way under the hood of my poncho and down my neck. He seemed to make a decision. "Take a break."

I followed him to the office. Dropped my backpack onto the chair by the door and pulled off my poncho.

"What dead guy?" he asked, low and level.

"The guy in the river."

"You already said that."

"It was in the newspaper. You didn't read about it?"

"I don't get the paper," he said with forced patience.

"Let me think," I said, pushing wet hair off my forehead. "First news about it was last week. Then a few days ago they said it was murder. They hadn't identified him yet. I've got the articles at home if you want to see." He looked at me, curious, so I explained. "Years ago, I did a school project about the river. Now, for whatever reason, I still save news and history and stuff. About the river, I mean."

Rat continued to gaze at me curiously. I looked away,

uncomfortable. He turned and headed to the back room. My eyes drifted automatically to the wall of bathing beauties. Then once again I noticed the black-and-white photograph on the bulletin board. The one of Rat and another guy doing trash duty. Flipper had said Unk worked here. That must be Unk. He'd also said, "Rat, he hate that guy." This time I noticed Rat wasn't smiling in the picture, but the taller guy was, one elbow playfully leaning on Rat's shoulder. I looked closer. The guy was holding something in his lower hand. A cap. Like the one from the river.

Rat returned with cups of coffee just as I was pulling the hat out of my pack. I held it up beside the picture.

"It's *his* hat," I said.

"What's *that*?" Rat asked.

"This hat. It's his hat," I repeated, still staring into the photo.

"THAT!" Rat demanded.

I looked at him, uncomprehending. Standing behind the desk, he set one coffee down and pointed at my backpack on the chair. The spiral notebook, which I had stuffed in without closing, had slipped partway out when I had pulled out the hat. Even upside down and from where he stood, it was easy to read, the way I had written it, with bold, block lettering.

RAT LIFE

I couldn't believe it! I stared at it as intently as Rat, like the sight was something bizarre. The office chair creaked when Rat sat, his eyes on me, waiting for an answer. I blushed enough to bleed from my ears, thinking again how every conversation I ever had with him seemed to take some abrupt wrong turn.

"That's . . . homework," I managed to say.

"Homework," he said flatly, making the word sound like some relic from a lost way of life.

"Uh . . . yeah, English class." I stared at my notebook, unable to meet his eyes. "Creative writing," I elaborated.

No response.

"See, I have to write a story—something historical. We've already had a couple different kinds of assignments. Now it's historical. You know. Fiction," I said, trailing off.

I looked up at Rat. He waited for more.

"I've been having trouble with the assignments. I like to write. Well, I used to. Lately I don't know. I guess I was thinking . . ." I took a deep breath. Let it out. "You know . . . about the Vietnam War. Maybe I'd write about that. And since you . . . mentioned it, maybe I could . . . ask you some questions."

I picked up the notebook and closed it. Felt ridiculous. Here was a guy who'd been to war and back. And here I was, a stupid kid wanting to write a little story about it for homework. I felt like a liar too. Because it wasn't the Vietnam War I was interested in. For some reason I couldn't completely understand, I wanted to know more about *him*. Maybe because there was that one thing that he knew about me, the one thing no one else in the world knew. The thing that happened beside the road. He understood that about me. Then he gave me a job. Flipper had said, "Rat, he work alone." If that was true, why did he want me working with him?

What had my plan been? To worm some information out of him and write it secretly? Probably. Actually, I had no plan. As usual.

"Wanna know if I killed any babies?" His voice was bitter. He stared at me. Hard.

"No!" I blurted, but it came out too quick. As if I was covering something. I did know kids who made cracks like that. As if everyone in the military was exactly that—a baby killer. At Elmore College, war protesters built fires in the streets, burned flags and draft cards. Once, a picture in the paper showed three students with a man-sized rag doll dressed in army fatigues. They were throwing it into the flames.

But just because I wasn't a war protester didn't mean I had nothing to hide from Rat's gaze. I wasn't sure if I was for or against it. I didn't personally know anyone else who had gone off to the war. No one I knew had dodged the draft. It didn't seem like the war had anything to do with me. Just bad luck if you got caught up in it. I remembered Rat's words, back when I first met him. Talking about me finding the pup, he had said, "Luck of the draw, sometimes." That was Vietnam to me—just an unlucky card to draw.

Somehow I held his gaze. "I don't think that," I said. "I . . . I don't know what to think."

He stared at me a long time. Finally, quietly, he said, "I remember . . ." His eyes dropped to his coffee. "I flew into San Francisco, coming back from Nam. Only been out of the boonies seemed like a few days. I wasn't counting. Came in on a real plane. You know, a commercial job. Me in uniform. With all these civilians. People wouldn't look at me. I'm lugging my bag to some bus stop outside the terminal. I pass a family with a bunch of kids—all standing around a stack of luggage. They see me. And turn away. Except one kid, about your age. He's kinda bored, just watchin' me. Then like it's nothing at all, he gives me the finger."

It was the most Rat had ever spoken at one time. At last I knew exactly what I thought. "That sucks."

24

". . . so, the first movie is over. There are two more to go. Mr. Huber calls it the Summer Triple Creature Feature. Did I already say that? Three monster movies!"

"Summer?" Leaky asked, looking up at me. He had ridden over on his bike after we'd come home from church and joined us for Sunday dinner. Now he was draped across my bed, while I paced around the room describing last night, my second night of work.

"It's not summer yet, I know, but they wanted to do this thing while the college kids were still in town. So anyhow. During intermission between the first two movies, Mr. Huber mans the ticket booth. Rat takes me out back to the snack bar. Says we have to do a stunt. See, the second movie is about people turning into radioactive monsters. And our advertisement promised real monsters in the theater."

Leaky said, "You got the job 'cause you don't need a mask."

"Funny. As I was saying, we go into the projection room. Inside, it's all dark and the walls are painted black.

There's these two big projectors, floor to ceiling. One is playing the intermission film advertising snack bar food."

"Yea-a-ah," said Leaky. "Dancing hot dogs make me hungry."

"I thought you gave up hot dogs forever. Anyhow, the projectionist, Bill, he's busy getting the second movie started. He's saying, 'Don't touch anything, blah, blah, blah.' Once the movie's rolling, Bill pulls out a box full of costumes that came with the movie. We gotta wear the stuff. I'm thinking this is stupid, but Rat's doing it, like it's just another job. So. We get dressed. We're each wearing a full head mask with ratty hair and melting skin. Big rubber hands too, covered with oozing sores. We got humps on our backs and grungy raggedy clothes. Bill's telling what's gonna happen. About twenty-five minutes into the movie, we'll hear people screaming. That's our signal to go outside and do our monster show. You know, run around and scare little kids."

Leaky groaned. "Man! I miss *all* the good stuff."

"Wait. Here's where it gets cool. First we're supposed to get our costumes charged up with light. We do a test. Bill positions us by the machine rolling the movie, and he shows us a drawing on an instruction sheet. We're supposed to close our eyes and hold our hands in front of our faces, palms out . . ."

I showed Leaky the position as I was describing it.

" . . . then cover our eyes with the backs of our fingers. Bill says cover up as little of the mask as possible. When we're in position, he says, 'Ready?' He turns away and opens a side panel of the projector. This blazing bright light is burning in there. So bright, I swear, even with my eyes shut and covered by my hands, I can see the bone shadows of my fingers. He counts to five and closes the machine. When the spots in my eyes clear, I look at Rat. He's glowing green! And what I can see of my own costume looks pretty cool too, I must admit.

"Rat and I start doing Frankenstein at each other while Bill loads the next movie reel. We wait. After a few minutes our glow fades out. This time it's for real. Bill's listening. As soon as we hear people screaming, he yells, 'Ready!' We get in position. He opens the projector and we get blasted with light for a five count. He slams it shut and throws open the side door. Rat and I tear out into the parking lot.

"I'm still kinda blinded at that point. I can't see where I'm going and *WHAM,* I fall over the hood of someone's car. The guy yells and I jump back. I keep running, looking for Rat. It's dark except for the light from the movie. There's a lotta cars, considering it rained until almost showtime. But there's empty spaces too. And a lot of the unused speakers are on. They're blaring all over the place. So I'm surrounded by movie screams. I look up at the movie and sure enough, there's a bunch of glowing, dissolving people just like me.

"I see Rat a couple rows away running kinda like a chimpanzee, kinda like a zombie. He comes up in front of a car, raises both glowing hands, roars, then slaps the hood and keeps going. I take a row behind him and do the same. The more I do it, man, the more I get into it. And after making a few little kids scream, I *really* get into it. I do a couple rows. Suddenly the screams stop because, in the movie, it's now the next day or something. I look at my hands and the glow is pretty much gone, so I jog back to the projection room. Rat gets there about the same time. I start pulling off my costume but Bill says 'Whoa! You got two more curtain calls. Just sit tight.'

"Ten minutes later Bill says get ready. The screaming starts. We get hit with the light again, then we're out the door. We head for the cars in back because we didn't get them the first time.

"So I'm doing my thing, slapping cars and growling, until I realize I'm at the very last row and there's only one car. I haven't seen Rat for a while. So I do the car. I slap the hood. Growl. Start to head back to the snack bar. The car windows are down and I hear a girl giggle. A guy starts swearing. Guy yells, 'Hey, you turd!' Then he says, 'You wanna see something *real* scary?'

"Like a fool I stop—a few parking spaces away. I look back. 'Come'ere,' he says, nicer sounding. Without think-ing, I take a step his way. He says, 'Check out my knife.' I freeze in my tracks. Because the guy's opening his door. A beer bottle spills onto the ground. The movie speaker falls and dangles around the pole. He climbs out. Girl says, 'Barry, don't.' But he's somehow unbelievably pissed and he raises one arm toward me, something in his hand. The movie screaming has stopped now. It's quiet. I hear this *SNICK* and a knife blade flashes in his hand.

"I start backing away, but I can't take my eyes off that knife. I back up against a speaker pole and trip over the concrete base. Fall on my butt! Guy's only about a car space away. That knife looks like a sword. Then the girl cries, 'Barry!' just as I hear a *THUNK* sound. Guy goes, 'What . . . ?' and looks back. It's Rat. His mask is off. He had just slapped the hood of the car. The whole place is quiet and I hear Rat say in a normal voice, 'Boo, asshole.'"

"Da-a-a-amn," Leaky whispered.

"So the guy goes for Rat. Rat steps away from the car, pulling the monster gloves off his hands. Me, I'm totally freaked. I run for the snack bar. Then I realize I'm leaving Rat all alone. Then I think—he can handle it 'cause he was in the army. But I stop, because no way should I leave him. I look back, but now there's several rows between me and the back row and all I can see are cars. I don't see Rat or anybody.

"So I'm wondering what I should do, when I hear some little kid in a car nearby say, 'He ain't scary no more.' I look and a whole carload of kids are watching me. I'm not glowing anymore. One of them makes a face at me. Then I look up and there's Rat. All cool and calm. We go back to the projection room and I'm asking, 'What happened?' He shakes his head for me to be quiet. Tells Bill, 'We're done for tonight.' Bill starts in about one more monster run, but we take off our stuff and leave."

I stopped. Leaky let out a breath. "That was goo-o-o-d. Your best yet!"

"What?" I asked.

"Your story," he said. "It sounded so real!"

I stared at him for a second. He thought I'd made it up! I turned and from my bottom desk drawer I pulled out what looked like a short magician's wand with silver tips. I pointed it at Leaky, pushed a button, and out snicked a gleaming six-inch blade.

"A gift from Rat," I said.

25

Leaky turned the knife over. Closed it. Clicked it open. "Man! Why can't I work for someone with a name like Rat?"

"You hate work," I answered.

"Oh, right. I forgot."

"I have something else to show you." With my toe I nudged the hat I'd been carrying in my pack. It was on the floor by the dresser, drying out. "I found that in the river a few days ago."

"Yeah, well, throw it back," Leaky said, barely glancing at it. He was slashing and stabbing the air with my knife.

I don't know why I even mentioned the hat. Maybe I was trying to figure out something for myself. I said, "The weird thing was when I showed it to Rat. I was going to ask him about the military insignia on it. Since he was in Vietnam and all."

"*Vietnam?*" Leaky gave me a bug-eyed look.

"Anyway," I went on, "Rat sees the hat and gets . . . I don't know . . . weird. Won't talk about it."

"That's weird all right," Leaky said sarcastically. "Who *wouldn't* want to talk about such an interesting thing?"

"But there's something else," I persisted. Leaky wasn't paying attention, so I held out my hand until he gave me the knife. "I found a picture on a bulletin board at the drive-in office. A snapshot—of a guy working with Rat. The guy was holding this hat. I think he's one of Rat's mom's boyfriends."

"O-o-oh. The plot thickens." Leaky leered, then added, "Wait, back up. Someone named Rat actually has a mom?"

I ignored him. "I haven't met the guy. I heard he hasn't been around for a couple weeks. Then I remembered— that dead guy showed up in the river a couple weeks ago." Leaky's eyes darted to the hat on the floor as I continued. "I had joked to Rat that it would be cool if the hat belonged to the guy they found in the river. It would be, you know, evidence. That's when Rat acted so weird."

"Okay! Wait! Let me guess," Leaky said gleefully. "Rat hates his mom's boyfriend. Kills the guy. Throws him in the river. Now you find the hat and solve the murder!"

"You're twisted."

"Just kidding, man. If you didn't want to talk about it, why'd you mention it? You're the one said Rat was in Vietnam. Those guys are psycho."

"Yeah, you know so much about it!"

"I know my dad won't hire Vietnam vets. Says they're ticking time bombs. Not cool, man!"

I had no reply to that. Why *had* I mentioned it? I suddenly felt sick—felt like I had betrayed Rat by talking about him. But worse—Leaky's little murder theory was exactly what I had been trying not to think about. No way could I believe it, but once the idea showed up, I couldn't quite shake it either.

What *did* I know about Rat? Not much. I was certain he couldn't be much older than me. But he seemed to know things. Could take care of himself.

He was a soldier.

So did that mean he was a killer? Maybe not. Maybe he wasn't on the front lines. I just didn't know. He didn't talk much. That story about the kid giving him the finger—for Rat, it had been a major speech. But that had been the end of it.

I pulled out my desk drawer and buried the knife in some junk. I pulled out a box and kicked the drawer shut. "Hey, I almost forgot. Check this."

"Fa-a-r-r-r out, man!" Leaky's eyes opened so wide, they could have rolled out of his head.

It was an old wooden cigar box with all the paper labels removed. Someone had drawn on the wood surface with ballpoint pens—blacks, blues, and reds, looking exactly like tattoo art. On the lid was a motorcycle with a naked babe riding it. Clouds of smoke boiled up everywhere. The smoke turned into ogres and beasts that spilled down the sides of the box while flames licked up from below. The bottom was covered with fire. In the center, emerging from flames, was a devilish grinning face.

Leaky stuttered, "Did . . . did you . . . ?"

"Get real! I can't draw like this. I found it in one of the rooms last week."

I didn't think he needed details. Truth was, it had been left by the drunk guy. Dad had thrown his stuff out, but the box, under the bed, got overlooked. Everything inside it—the guy's dope—I flushed down the toilet. I finished cleaning the room, locked up, and took the box. Next morning that room was busted wide open. It was trashed. Dad said the guy still had a key so he changed the locks. He thought it was revenge, but I knew better. The guy had been looking for his stash. I didn't tell Dad about the box because . . . well . . . I wanted to keep it.

Leaky held the box gently, reverently. Studied every detail.

Through my bedroom window I saw Rat pull into the driveway on his bike.

"He's here," I said.

"Who?"

"Rat. I wonder what he wants." I grabbed the box, stuffed it quickly under my pillow, and hurried out the door.

Leaky followed. "Hey, I better be . . . I gotta get going."

Rat's bike was leaning against the "Vacancy" sign and he was just walking up to the office door. Leaky pushed past me and picked up his own bike.

"What's happening?" I said to Rat. Then, "Hey, Leaky, I want you to meet—"

"Cool! Hi." Leaky waved, not making eye contact. He abruptly rode off. Weird!

Rat looked at me. "Leaky?"

"It's a long story."

"Well . . ." He looked uncomfortable. His hands were stuffed in his pockets. "I just wondered if you could help me with that wood."

It had rained yesterday afternoon and we never carried the lumber down to the river. "Okay. I'll ask Mom. I have to fix a few lawn chairs. But after that . . ."

"Great." He glanced around, then looked through the open office door. He seemed nervous.

"Where's the truck?" I asked.

"My mother has it. But I unloaded the wood in the backyard. So, you really do live at a motel."

It was a strange thing to say. He'd been here before. Thinking he was trying to be funny, I answered, "So? You live at a drive-in!"

"No, it's cool. I didn't mean . . ." He left it hanging.

I was confused. My reply had been in jest, but it seemed to leave him fumbling for words, looking everywhere but at me. Definitely nervous.

"You want to write about Vietnam?" He was gazing out at the road when he asked. The question surprised me. Before I could answer, Leaky's words whispered to me.

Ticking time bomb psycho.

Was that why Leaky tore out of here when Rat arrived? More importantly, *did* I want to write about Vietnam?

Yesterday I had told Rat I didn't know how I felt about the war. But last night, trying to fall asleep, I realized— I did have an opinion. It must have formed without my even knowing. Of course I didn't like the war. But beyond that? All the news over the years—the protests, the body counts, the burning villages—had gradually piled up on me. If I were under oath, I'd have to say I thought my country was wrong to be in the war. When I had asked Rat about his tattoo and he'd said, "Vietnam," I realized now—that word changed things. How could it not? When I thought about it, the very word itself, *Vietnam,* sounded evil. Poisonous. Was Rat a part of that? Was he tainted by it? Did I really want to know?

I shrugged and stammered, "I . . . I . . . guess."

Rat snorted a short laugh. "Well, that's inspiring." He shook his head. Looked at his feet. Then it hit me why Rat was nervous. He was saying he was willing to talk. He had opened a door. And I had hesitated. And already that door was closing. If I really did want to know more—and suddenly I did—I had to think of something. Now. But what?

I said, "Can I show you something I wrote?"

20

Rat was a slow reader, working laboriously down each page. I stood at the window. I paced. I threw darts at my board.

When I had handed him the pages, I immediately wished I hadn't. I felt exposed, probably like he had just felt when he asked if I wanted to write about Vietnam. Then it occurred to me that I couldn't imagine sharing this particular piece of writing with anyone else but him. Suddenly I couldn't wait to hear what he thought. Then I worried that I should have maybe improved it some, knowing Rat would be the reader. No, I decided. It was better this way. By the time he finished, I was back to regretting it.

He sat on the edge of my desk, looking down at the papers for a while, then said, "That was a tough thing." Said it in a low voice like he was talking to himself—like he wasn't talking about the pup at all, but something else entirely. Finally, he said the only words that really mattered. "You got it right."

Then silence. Like after a blessing. I took in his words, knowing that Rat, in his way, was saying he liked it. But more, he was saying something about the writing. About its rightness. No one had ever made a comment like that before. Because I'd never written like that before.

But as the silence continued—and it may have only been a few seconds—I got nervous again. What if, now, he agreed to tell me his story? How could I possibly write about Rat in Vietnam? Okay, so I wrote about a pup dying on the side of the road. But Vietnam? How could I capture the rightness in that? How could I do his story justice, whatever it might be. I should have just pulled out an encyclopedia and written about something regular. Roman gladiators. The Alamo. *Anything* but Vietnam.

Feeling a little dazed by my own roller-coaster thinking, I abruptly sat down on the bed, partially on my pillow, and felt a lump. I had forgotten the box under there. I pulled it out.

Rat dropped my papers on the desk and shot to his feet. "Where did you get that?" He lunged at me, took it from my hands. "Where'd you get this?" he demanded.

Startled, I couldn't get my words out. "I . . . the guy . . ."

"WHO?"

"The guy . . . in his room."

"WHAT GUY?" I must have looked pretty freaked out, because he backed off. "Okay, sorry," he said, but still urgent. "Just tell me. What guy? When?"

"That guy. Remember I told you? The guy who smashed up the drink machine? It was in his room. When Dad threw him out, he threw out all his stuff. But he missed the box. So, when I cleaned up the room, I found it under the bed."

Rat groaned.

"Why?" I said nervously. "What is it?"

He went to my window and looked up and down the highway like the guy might be out there. He turned and held the box between us. "This belongs to my so-called father."

Rushing out the door, I almost collided with Mom. "Oh, hey," I said, "I was just coming to look for you."

"Did I see . . . Rat? Leaving on a bike?" She still had a hard time saying his name.

"Yeah. He rides it when his mom has the truck. Look, can I go out to work early? He needs my help with something."

"The paper said possible thunderstorms this afternoon," she answered.

"I'll take an extra shirt, just in case. Thanks, Mom!"

She called after me, "Fix those chairs first, like your father asked."

When I thought about it, having a job away from home made me feel different. "Self-reliant," Dad might say. The surprising thing was that Dad actually seemed okay about the job. Sure, he was going out of his way to load me up with chores—like, what's the big emergency to fix a couple lawn chairs?—but I was keeping up. Plus, I was handling the rabies shots on my own. All in all, I felt more freedom to come and go. They were trusting me!

At the thought of their trust, the switchblade came to mind, and the stash box, both hidden in my drawer. And I wondered what they would think about me hanging around with a Vietnam vet. I hadn't mentioned *that* either. But I avoided those thoughts like bullies on a playground.

When the chairs were done I got ready to go. I grabbed an extra shirt and stuffed it in my pack, which was still damp from the last rain. It occurred to me that it had been raining for-freakin'-ever! Mom watched the weather because so much motel work took her outside. She also kept an eye on Florida, where *her* mom and dad live. A few days ago she'd mentioned a hurricane. I wondered if a hurricane in Florida could have anything to do with rainy weather in New York. Not likely.

I double-checked that the knife and the box were well buried in my drawer. I took another look at that amazing box.

Rat's father? I *had* to start writing stuff down!

I opened my notebook to the words *Rat Life*. Under them, I wrote:

(Rat) This belongs to my so-called father.

I closed it and started wrapping it in my poncho to keep it dry.

But I couldn't let it go, didn't want to forget anything. Even though Rat was waiting for me, I sat down on the edge of my bed, unwrapped the notebook, and wrote down everything he had said as fast as I could.

RAT LIFE

(Rat) This belongs to my so-called father.

(T) What do you mean?

(silence)

(T) You mean the guy that hassled me and Gram? He's your father?

(more silence)

(T) Did he draw that? The stuff on the box?

(R) (laughs) Hell, no! He probably stole it. But he's had it ever since I can remember.

(silence)

(R) I thought he was in prison.

(silence)

(R) Must be out. Guess he found us.

(long silence)

(T) You're sure it's him? Big guy. Driving this puke-green car. Like a Chrysler or something. That sound right?

(R) Don't know about a car. I haven't seen him since I went into the army. Three years ago. (short laugh) My fourteenth birthday.

(T) (stunned silence)

(more silence)

(T) I'm fourteen.

(silence)

(T) You went into the army . . . you were . . . my age?

(R) Your age? I was never your age.

(silence)

(R) When I was your age . . . I was no age at all. I was nothing. Being some age? Doesn't mean anything if there's nobody to be that age for.
(silence)

(R) Know how they say, "He's tall for his age"? Or they say, "Oh my, he's already five!" But when there's nobody there to say it, you're nothing. You're not any age. You're not tall or short. (looks out the window) Nothing matters if you're nothing. I wasn't part of any of it. Streets. Houses. None of it!

School. (short laugh) School. I didn't know one grade from another. I was just there. I didn't do shit. It didn't mean shit. It was just a place that was away from some dirty, half-empty house. School was . . . school was a hole. I hid in it. Everybody above me just walking by.
(silence)

(R) Got to where I didn't even look up.

27

Mom had been right about a storm. I rode out to the theater beneath a heavy gray sky. We had to get that wood hauled quickly. As I rode, I kept seeing the raging drunk guy in the doorway of Cabin 12. "Dad?" I said aloud, trying to put myself in Rat's place. I couldn't begin to imagine it. Instead, the fear I had felt that day—the hate that had flamed up out of nowhere—came back to me in an instant. I saw Gram in that filthy car. Saw the guy's bleary red face yelling at us. I got jaw-clenching angry all over again. Then a question hit me so suddenly, my bike wobbled. Had Rat lived his whole life feeling like this?

I found him behind his house. The scrap lumber was on the ground, sorted into lengths, and he was pulling nails from a few used boards. "Hey," said Rat. "Here ya go." He tossed a second claw hammer my way. I dropped my bike and joined him. When the boards were clean we started hauling armloads at a time. It took three trips down to the river. The underbrush was wet from last night's rain. My sneakers and pants legs were quickly soaked. In some places the ground was marshy, with pools of water in low spots. We stacked the lumber on a high part of the bank beneath the tree house.

Rat seemed preoccupied. He never started his usual work banter.

I looked at the high platform. Getting the wood up there was going to be a miserable job.

Rat must have read my mind. "Let's take five."

I followed him up the tree, glad to leave the lumber behind. For me the climb was slow, my arms weary and belly sore. When I got to the top deck, Rat was taking a seat on the edge out over the river, with a jar of drinking water. I joined him, hoping he would talk more about his father. But I didn't know how to get him started.

What question can I ask that won't blow up in my face? I wondered.

Rain began pattering through the leaves. It felt good after the hard work. A light breeze turned to wind and drops began slanting in harder. Suddenly it was too late to ask Rat any questions. The weather rapidly became amazing.

The wind rose dramatically. A deluge of giant pelting raindrops—what Dad Clampett would call "a real toad strangler"—drove us to shelter under the tarps. Lightning flashed and the rumble of thunder quickly followed.

Being that high up in the middle of a thunderstorm was exhilarating—at first. Wind and rain cut through the trees in an excited rush. Thunder rumbled and the sky flickered, making the already dark afternoon feel darker. Large masses of blowing leaves thrashed around us.

They seemed sculptural when freeze-framed by lightning. Below, sheets of rain chased over the river's surface.

It grew worse. Wind-driven rain hissed angrily through the trees. Thunder rolled almost continuously, punctuated by jarring detonations seemingly right above us. Below, small whitecaps blew upstream as if even the river was fleeing the storm's onslaught. A tarp ripped away from two of its corners, whipped and popped, then tangled itself in branches. The deck creaked as the trees swayed. There was a crack like a gunshot overhead. Silhouetted for an instant in lightning, a limb thicker than my leg plunged diagonally across our view not ten feet in front of us. Its branches slapped the deck where we had sat moments ago.

"That's it for me," Rat yelled.

He pushed me to the ladder and I scrambled down. By the time Rat jumped off the steps I was already jogging away. With the blowing rain, flashing lightning, and pools of water to avoid, I quickly lost my bearings. All I knew was to head uphill. Rat trailed behind me and I figured he wouldn't let me go too far astray. The rain-saturated air was filled with flying leaves, clumps of leaves, falling branches full of leaves. Up ahead, I saw a tree blow over, right into my path. I couldn't even hear it hit over the noise of the storm.

Geez! Get me the hell outta here!

Jogging around the freshly upturned roots, I crested a rise and stopped. Rat came up beside me. We faced a chain-link fence. Instead of coming out of the woods behind Rat's house, we had emerged at the back of the theater parking lot.

"There!" Rat pointed. A stone's throw away, a tree lay across the fence, crushing it to the ground. We raced to the spot and scrambled over. Crossed the open lot, splashing through rivers of water in the valleys between parking rows. Curtains of rain stung my face and blurred my vision. But the flicker of lightning and roll of thunder was growing distant. As quickly as the storm had hit, it began to diminish. By the time we got to the office the worst of the wind had passed and the rain fell nearly straight down.

Rat unlocked the office door. The power was out. From the pitch-dark bathroom, he brought out a bundle of paper towels. We almost used them all up getting dry. I felt myself begin to relax as we sat in the dim office and caught our breath.

Rat ribbed me. "Man, you 'bout got us lost in the woods."

"Yeah? Well, I noticed you were leading from the rear."

"Like all good officers!" He grinned.

A car horn sounded outside. We sat a moment in silence. It honked again, more insistent. Rat pushed himself to his feet. "Damn!" he muttered. "We don't even open for a couple hours."

I felt too weary to move but pushed myself up and followed. Outside the office door Rat's step faltered. A rusty green car idled in the driveway by the ticket booth, it's chrome grille nearly touching the painted sawhorse barricading the driveway. Rat probably didn't recognize the car like I did. But the driver was reaching across, rolling down the passenger window nearest us. He was easy to see.

"Howdy," the guy called with exaggerated friendliness. He stared only at Rat.

We just stood there in the rain. Getting wet again.

"I come to see the movie show," he said. And grinned. It was like a punch to my gut. Because his smile looked exactly like Rat's.

"Wha'sa matter? You *do* work here, don't you?"

Rat didn't answer.

"Am I early?" The guy smiled again. "I don't mind waiting. Won't hurt nothin'." He waggled a dollar bill out the window.

I surprised myself and spoke. "There's no power. We'll be closed tonight."

He squinted and finally recognized me. "Well, hey there, little buddy. How's that piss-pot granny of yours?"

Anger threatened to choke me, but I managed to repeat, "We're closed."

His face made a cartoon of disappointment. He dropped the dollar onto the ground. Pointed a finger at me, his hand like a pistol that recoiled when he silently shot me. He straightened. In slow motion, the car eased forward and toppled the barricade. Wood splintered. The car rolled over the pieces and into the theater. Without a word, we followed at a walk. Watched the car slowly cruise the entire circumference of the theater. With no change of speed, Rat's father continued out the exit on the far end of the screen building. I barely heard the crunch of the other sawhorse barricade. Then the squeal of accelerating tires. He was gone.

Rat turned and gave me a long look. Said, "That was good. About being closed tonight."

I shrugged. "I'm a writer. I make stuff up."

We walked back to the front. The power in the office was, of course, still out. "Actually," said Rat, looking at the driving rain, "we probably *will* be closed tonight."

"So, what about . . . ?" I started, but hesitated.

"My father?" Rat finished for me.

I shrugged. "Yeah, I mean, that's the guy, right?"

"That's the guy."

"What's he want?" I asked. "What are you going to do?"

There was a pause. Then he said, "Go home."

I wasn't sure if he meant *he* was going home or if he was telling *me* to go. Either way, I knew the end of a Rat conversation when I heard one.

───────

Back at the motel, Mom was dragging branches onto a pile in the yard. Dad was on the roof of Cabin 3, patching where it had been hit by the tree lying across our driveway. Tired and wet as I was, I found a saw and went to work.

That night, the power still out, I sat at my desk with a candle and a new, dry notebook from the office supply closet. And though my hands burned with blisters from sawing tree limbs, I wrote it all down, as much as I could remember. The rain and lightning. The incredible, mindless strength of the wind. Rat and his father. The fear.

Power came back on sometime after midnight. I was

still writing, but my brain felt like mush. I blew out the candle and went to sleep. My dreams were of storm-tossed trees. Rat was showing me how to lean into the wind and fly like a kite. I yelled above the storm for him not to do it. He spread his arms. Wind lifted him off the ground. I reached up and grabbed the front of his shirt. It flashed like lightning, so bright, I could see the bone shadows in my fingers. It burned. I let go. Rat flew away.

28

At breakfast the next day Mom was reading the paper, all about the storm. She said the weather experts claimed it was caused by that Florida hurricane, which, by the way, missed Grandma and Papa down south, but was now stalled over Pennsylvania.

It was going to be an especially painful Monday. I ached from hauling lumber and sawing limbs. My hands were dotted with slivers and blisters. I had only gotten a few hours of sleep. And—have I mentioned lately?—it was raining.

The school day was a blur. I couldn't stop thinking about the storm that Rat and I had survived. I kept recalling details I had forgotten to write down last night. Or thought of ways to rewrite parts I had already put on paper.

Leaky cut through my mental fog for a minute outside Hagerwood's class. In the hall he waved me close. "Check it out," he said, whipping his hand from his pocket and pointing something at me.

I couldn't believe my eyes. Was that the knife Rat gave me? "How did you . . ." I grabbed it from him just as I heard it go *SNICK*. "Are you nuts?" I yelled, then saw what I was holding—a handle with a silvery plastic fine-tooth comb sticking out. It said "Myrtle Beach, South Carolina" on the grip. I slapped the cheap souvenir back into his hand. "You are such a jerk!"

"Yeah," he said, dragging the comb through his hair, "but I look good."

As soon as Hagerwood's class got seated and quiet, my mind went straight back to the storm and the drive-in. And Rat.

And Rat's father.

Guess he found us.

That's what Rat had said. Like he and his mom were hiding from him. And speaking of his mom, where was she all this time? I hadn't seen her much. Hadn't seen Rat's uncle either. He was gone. I had his job. And his hat. The hat had been downstream from where the dead guy washed up about two weeks ago. When exactly was it? I had that newspaper clipping at home somewhere.

Rat, he hate that guy.

That's what Flipper had said about Unk. I still refused to believe Rat could have killed someone, even though I had nothing to go on except that I just didn't want it to be true.

How's that piss-pot granny of yours?

I felt sick with hate whenever I thought about Rat's father. And he hadn't even been involved with my life for more than a few minutes total! Out of morbid curiosity, I added up the minutes, starting when I found Gram in his car. Then watching him argue with Dad and smash the drink machine. Then at the theater. Maybe, just *maybe,* I'd been around the motel office back when he first checked in. I didn't remember. I don't pay much attention to most customers . . .

Wait. When did he first check in?

Wait a minute! When did the dead guy show up?

I was suddenly heart-poundingly awake.

Could the father . . . ? Could he have murdered Rat's "uncle"?

I actually felt light-headed from the idea, from the sudden rearrangement of puzzle pieces.

So, prove it, Sherlock!

But how . . . ? Hey! Maybe I *could* prove it! I knew one place to start looking.

29

When school let out that afternoon, I raced for home on my bike. It seemed to take forever. There had been no change in the weather except that rain had turned to heavy rain. Streets flowed with runoff. In some places, water gushed up around the edges of manhole covers. I hardly noticed, though. I had one thought. Proof! Waiting at home.

I swerved into the driveway. Dropped my bike and hit the door running. It seemed to hit back, I was so surprised by it being locked. I fumbled out my keys and opened it.

Behind the check-in desk we keep a long file box of five-by-seven registration cards. Everybody who'd stayed here this year was in the box. I thumbed back to last Friday, the day my drink machine got killed. One guy had checked in the night before, paying for two nights. Normally, customers filled out the cards. But for some reason, this one was in Mom's handwriting. The name: "John Fogerty."

That sounded familiar. But I didn't even know Rat's last name. Or his real first name, for that matter!

Below the name and address lines there were spaces for "Make of car," "Color," "License #," and "State." For make of car, Mom had written "Sedan." She wasn't what Dad would call a car person. For color she wrote "Green."

That had to be the guy who smashed the drink machine and left the stash box! Rat's father! Had to be!

Okay, I told myself, *back up.* When exactly was the dead guy found in the river?

I looked on the wall calendar. Mom wrote little notes on each day—a mini-log of our family history. "Todd to the emergency room" was written for Thursday, June 8. I was certain that Thursday was the day Leaky first mentioned the dead guy. I flipped back through the registration cards to that Thursday. Nothing but normal customers. Back to Wednesday. Nothing unusual. Tuesday. Nothing! A whole week back. Nothing!!! I went through them again. Zilch. I checked the calendar again. I looked around the room as if an explanation might be somewhere in plain sight. I flopped into the swivel chair behind the desk. Realized I was still wearing my dripping poncho. I flung it off angrily. Rainwater sprayed everywhere.

I was so sure that the evil father guy had to have been here once before, back when Unk disappeared.

It went something like this: Evil Father gets out of prison. Tracks down his loving family somehow. Cruises into scenic Elmore. Takes a room at the lovely Oak Acres Court. Spies on Rat and Weird Mom. Discovers Unk. Knocks off Unk. Dumps him in the river. Leaves town to let the dust settle. Rat doesn't know anything because he's off working on his tree house or something. Rat figures that when Unk doesn't show for work it just means he up and split town. No one's really surprised; the guy was a flake. Rat hires me. Weird Mom is all depressed about Unk disappearing. She stops showing up for work too. Meanwhile, Evil Father lets things cool down. Comes back to town. Checks in again at his favorite motel. To do what? Claim his woman? Have a family picnic? WHAT?

If all of that was true, then where was his first registration card? Actually, just because he didn't stay HERE back when the dead guy got dead didn't mean he didn't do it. It just meant I didn't have the evidence I thought I had. He could have stayed anywhere.

Then again, maybe I was wrong. Heck, maybe Rat's mom could have . . .

Whoa, that was it! Weird Mom—she killed Unk! That's why she'd been so weird lately and hadn't been around much.

But, nah. How was she going to drag a body through the woods and dump it in the river? Besides, if she did something like that, wouldn't she also split town?

Then, of course, Leaky could be right. About Rat.

Psycho.

No! I flat-out refused to believe . . .

That's when I spotted a note folded so that it would stand up. It was on the check-in desk. Right in front of me. On any other day I would have noticed it as soon as I came in. I picked it up. Mom's handwriting on the outside screamed, "TODD!"

Hold on a second. Why was the office door locked?

I opened the note, knowing it was bad news.

Todd,

We're at the hospital with Gram. Emergency. No time to explain. Sit tight. We'll call.

Love, Mom

That slammed me back to reality—Gram was sick. I went to the door and dumbly looked out to see for myself. Cabin 1 was dark. Mom's car was gone. Out front, the "No Vacancy" sign was lit and a "Closed" sign hung under it for good measure. I had come home and missed all that!

Then I realized I'd also missed my rabies shot! How could I have forgotten my shot? Where was my head?

Off somewhere inventing murder mysteries, that's where!

I walked back to my room. Did what I often do when I can't figure myself out. I stared into the dresser mirror. At a moron! I looked at all the moron junk on the moron's dresser. Pencils, papers, miniature chess set, tennis ball, model rocket. I swung the back of my hand. Swept everything off. It scattered across the floor. One thing fluttered: a newspaper clipping, landing lightly on the filthy green hat on the floor. The headline taunted me—"Body Found in Chemanga River." I picked it up. It was the first article. The date of the paper was in the corner. Friday. And the body had been found Thursday morning. That's when I saw the cops at Fischer's Bridge.

I read it again top to bottom. One detail jumped out. A policeman said he was no expert but figured the body had been in the river "well over a week"!

I had only searched registration cards that went back one week past Thursday. I hurried to the front desk. To the card file. Started flipping back again, card by card. One week back. Nothing, of course. Then I started going through cards I hadn't already checked. Ten days back. Twelve days. Still nothing. Two weeks. At eighteen days, I came to a smudged card, with hand-lettering so bad, I could barely read it.

NAME: John Fogerty

I went right to the car information.

MAKE OF CAR: CrAP
COLOR: CrAP GrEEn

I actually laughed. That had probably made Mom mad. Which would explain why she had personally filled out his second registration card when he returned three weeks later. She would definitely have remembered him.

Suddenly I knew why the name sounded familiar. John Fogerty, the singer from Creedence Clearwater Revival! Was this a fake name?

Never mind all that! This was the guy! And he was in town "well over a week" before the body showed up. To put it plainly, he was HERE when his wife's boyfriend was murdered!

Maybe it meant nothing.

Maybe it meant everything!

I had to tell Rat.

30

I got an odd busy signal. Was phone service still down at the drive-in? If Rat had a home number, I didn't have it and it would probably be down too.

The note about Gram stared up at me from the desk. I called the hospital, asked for the emergency room. Got put on hold. While I waited I looked at the room-key board. Only one room occupied. This place was all but deserted. I could make a quick trip out to the theater, talk to Rat, and come right back home. No one would miss me. I put down the phone.

I hated the thought of going out into the downpour again but I threw on my poncho, locked up, and took off.

The perpetual light over the theater's office door was out. Still no power. I banged on the door. Nothing. Pulled at it. Locked as usual. I rode far enough into the theater to see the snack bar. It seemed adrift in the rain, dark and lifeless.

I pedaled back to Rat's driveway and coasted down to the house. Branches and clumps of leaves littered the ground from yesterday's storm. I could see enough of the backyard to tell the truck wasn't there. From the driveway I noticed that the screen door was open a couple inches.

"Rat!" I yelled, dropping my bike. I followed the walkway to the porch. The screen door was only screened on the upper half. Through it, I saw the inner door was also open, revealing blackness and silence. I stepped onto the porch.

"Rat," I called again. "You won't believe . . ."

Looking down, I saw a round dark object holding the screen door open.

" . . . what I . . ."

I pulled the door open.

". . . found . . ."

The dark thing in the doorway rotated a little. A lock of stiff hair shifted. I lurched away spastically, not believing my eyes. Words strangled in my throat.

A head! In the doorway.

A body!

I stumbled backward off the porch. Landed on my butt, tangled in my poncho.

The screen door creaked and lazily thunked back against . . . the head. In the nightmare moment that I had held the door open I had glimpsed the rest of the body angling crookedly into the dark room. And I had seen blood. A lot of blood!

"Oh, man!" I scrambled to my knees.

Was that . . . Rat? Did his dad . . .

No . . . not Rat. Couldn't be. The hair was too long.

"RAT!" I yelled, panicky. I stood. Wiped my hands on my jeans. Stepped up to the door again. Gingerly I pulled it open. The head didn't move this time. Not at all. Neither did the body. I stared hard at it. No sign of breathing. I could see enough of a profile—a hair-draggled cheek—to recognize Rat's father.

"Da-a-a-amn!" I whispered to no one.

Deeper in the room a candle guttered dimly from a dish on a cardboard box coffee table. A smear of blood on the floor trailed from the body back to a hallway. The guy had crawled out . . .

"I wish you hadn't come here."

I whirled around. Rat held a rifle, pointed vaguely at my knees. He didn't meet my gaze but looked past me, at the porch, the screen door. "You gotta come with me." I searched his face for a sign, desperate to believe that this was some kind of joke. He lifted the rifle, swung the barrel until it pointed to the woods. "This way."

I had to agree with him. I wished I hadn't come. What was I thinking?

31

"Now!" Rat's eyes flicked up to mine.

I came off the porch. He half-stepped backward. I brushed past him and stopped at my bike in the driveway.

"Take it around back." I pushed the bike and he followed. "Leave it." I dropped the bike. He pointed the rifle toward the river. "That way."

I can't really say why, but the rifle didn't scare me. I just couldn't make myself believe . . . I was sure he wouldn't . . . use it . . . on me.

But in truth, I had no way of knowing *what* he was capable of. Was he a ticking time bomb psycho? One thing was certain. His father was in the house, dead. I turned toward the river.

As soon as I started walking, I saw water-pooled tire tracks leading into the underbrush. I followed them, Rat close behind. I came to the crap-green car. It had been driven into the woods until it could go no farther, blocked by trees, its tires pressing into the rain-softened ground. We passed it in silence.

Soon after the car, we found ourselves walking in muck, then water. And not just pools in low spots. This water was ankle-deep and slowly flowing. I hesitated. Looked back at Rat.

"Go on," he said.

The muddy forest floor sucked my shoes off a couple times before I figured out how to lift my feet. I looked back at Rat, but he didn't seem in a hurry. Suddenly I stepped into knee-deep water. Felt a current tugging at my pants. I scanned ahead for familiar landmarks, but everything looked different. The contours of the sloping ground were leveled by water. Something bumped my leg. I stared, strangely fascinated, as a basketball bobbed away, weaving downstream through the trees.

It occurred to me that I'd been blind for days, dealing with rabies shots, the drive-in job, Rat's father, murder mysteries . . . and now Rat with a rifle. That basketball opened my stupid eyes to what was obvious. This was no longer just some inconvenient rain. The river was flooding. Big time!

And we were headed into it.

"Rat—"

"Go!" he cut me off. The urgency in his voice freaked me out even more.

"This place is flooding, man!" I yelled, looking ahead toward the river. "This is bad!"

"Not much farther." His voice was controlled again, determined.

I slogged on and water rose higher. Over my knees. Pulling at the bottom edges of my poncho. Finally the woods opened. With relief I recognized the cluster of trees that held Rat's tree house. The entire load of wood we had piled there was gone. Washed away.

I was nearly waist deep now and the current was strong. Though I couldn't see it, I knew the bank dropped off, down to the base of the huge tree where steps were nailed. I probed tentatively with one foot. Heard Rat say quietly, "Careful now." Which is exactly when I slipped down the submerged bank. My legs swept out from under me. I slammed against the tree, then was pushed past it. Something snagged my poncho. The neck of the hood caught under my chin, jerking me to a stop. Water gushed over my head and I went under, face up, grabbing at anything. I was being pulled back against the flow. My head came up, water sluicing over my shoulders. Rat had me by the corner of my poncho. I flailed about madly and caught a rung of the tree ladder. I wrestled against the torrent, finally got footing on a submerged step, and scrambled up out of the river.

I climbed to the top deck and crawled to the far side. Sat with my back against a tree trunk. I was trembling. Not from being cold or wet. Just shaking all over. Still feeling the powerful current that had almost washed me downriver. I yanked the poncho over my head and threw it aside. I was soaked underneath anyway, so what good was it? I pulled my knees to my chest to make a tight knot with no room for trembling.

Rat made his way onto the platform. He laid the rifle by the footlockers. Didn't look my way, but went to work overhead, restretching the tarps that had blown loose yesterday. He got half the deck sheltered again, out to the fire pit. He lifted the heavy steel sink from its hole in the deck and dumped sludgy ash from a previous fire. Dropped the sink back into place and filled it with dry kindling from a footlocker. With dry matches from a jar, he started a fire.

As soon as the blaze no longer needed coaxing, Rat started kicking the deck clear of yesterday's fallen branches and leaves. I stared in disbelief. He was housekeeping! His father dead in the living room. The river flooding. Me a hostage or something. And he's tidying up the stupid tree house?

"What are you doing?" I yelled, so angry, my voice cracked.

He didn't answer, just finished clearing the deck, then went to the second footlocker. With his back to me he said, "Come get dried off."

Where I sat was beyond the shelter of the tarps. I stood up, the fire between us. The fear I'd felt at the house, then down below in the water, was now completely replaced by anger. I didn't even feel the rain. "Tell me!" I demanded. "What happened back there? What are you . . . what are *we* doing here?"

Rat pulled off his wet shirt. From the footlocker he produced a tattered blanket. With two quick pulls he ripped it in half and dropped one piece onto the deck in my general direction. He dried off with his half, then tossed it behind him. He replied with a question. "What are *you* doing here?"

"Me?" I nearly shrieked. I looked down at the river, looked at the rifle. "This isn't exactly my idea."

His voice was low, forcibly patient. "Why did you come out here—to the drive-in?"

"ANSWER ME!" I screamed. "WHAT'S GOING ON? YOU KILLED YOUR FATHER! YOU HAVE A GUN ON ME! WHAT *IS* ALL THIS?"

I was shaking again. Beneath the drumming of my heart, beneath the hiss of the rain, there was another sound. A sound that rose even louder in Rat's silence. It was the deep churn of river water coursing through the woods. Above it all, my own words echoed in my head.

You killed your father!

You have a gun on me!

You! Killed! Your! Father!

32.

I didn't move. Just stared at him, waiting for an answer.

He gazed out at the river for a long time. Then looked down at the blanket by his feet. Nudged it toward me. It looked incredibly dry and I was *so* sick of being wet. But I stayed out in the rain, stubbornly insisting with my glare that he talk.

The fire was between us. He nudged the blanket again. Closer to me. Closer to the fire. The faintest whisper of a smile pulled at one corner of his mouth. I glanced down. Another push with his toe. A corner of the cloth flapped over the edge of the steel sink. It quickly started smoldering. More of a smile.

And I realized—Rat was messing with me, taunting me with the blanket. The gesture wasn't the kind of answer I was expecting. But suddenly he looked . . . I don't know—certainly not like a father-killer. Or a psycho. He just looked like the guy I had gotten to know at work, the guy who could pick up a piece of trash and joke about it.

A tongue of flame blossomed out of the smolder and spread up the cloth to the lip of the sink. He stepped back.

"Geez!" I said, and lunged around the fire. I kicked the blanket away from the sink and stomped the flaming corner. "Where we supposed to go if you burn this place down?"

"Go with the flow, man," he said, doing his impression of a stoned hippie. He spread his arms. "It's, like, the river of life. You know?"

"So jump in it, why don't you!" I pulled off my shirt and dried myself with the blanket.

Rat dropped to one knee and poked at the fire. I sat down under the tarps, blanket over my shoulders, glad to be out of the rain. Rat threw more wood into the sink, then jammed sticks upright between planks near the fire, where he hung our shirts to dry. We both sat staring into the flames.

Campfires during my brief Boy Scout career had usually made my mind wander. Not this time. Not with the gush of water below. Or with the trees vibrating—I began to feel it once I sat still, the rising river strumming the trunks below.

"You gotta tell me what's going on," I said.

He looked sidelong at me, then repeated, "Why did *you* come out here to the drive-in?"

I dropped my head onto my knees in frustration. I was making no progress at all with this conversation!

"I *mean*," he went on, "what was so important that you would come out to the theater in this weather?"

After finding a dead body, after nearly drowning in the river, my reason for coming felt like ancient history. "That guy . . ." I hesitated. "Your father? He, uh, he stayed at the motel."

"You told me already. He wrecked your drink machine."

"No, see, he stayed there once before." It suddenly seemed pointless. The guy was dead. But I went on. "Back, you know . . . weeks ago . . . before that body washed up from the river. I . . . I dug up that newspaper article about when they found the dead guy. A cop said the body'd been in the water quite a while. So I looked through our registration file and found . . . your father. He was at the motel back when the guy was killed. Used a fake name and everything."

"So you came to tell me—what? My father killed Unk?"

I felt myself blush. Couldn't look up from the flames, but I nodded.

Rat groaned, let out a breath. "Damn, Todd."

Neither of us spoke for a long time. In the silence I realized it was the first time he'd ever used my name.

At last, he started talking.

33

"You're right. The guy in the river? Was Unk. My father killed him. I didn't know 'til 'bout an hour ago.

"I'm sorry. I didn't realize . . . this flood, I mean. I'm sorry for bringing you out here.

"The rifle's empty. When you came, I was out back. I drove that car into the woods, outta sight. Was just headed down to the river to throw the rifle in. Then I heard you calling. So here we are. I'm sorry. I . . .

"My father . . . I watched him die. It took a while. I thought about you and that pup. How you had to kill it. The pain and all. But the rifle was empty. Guess I could have found a way to end him sooner. But he started talking. About Unk. So I just listened.

"He screwed with you pretty good. Guess you have a right to know about him. He was . . . he was a bastard. A monster. Ever since I was little he'd come and go. Long times I wouldn't see him at all. That was a problem for him. I mean, that I was little. Called me a little pissant. He smacked me around.

"But mostly? Mostly he was my mother's monster. I

don't really know how she survived. Except he wasn't ever around enough to kill her all the way.

"I always made him mad. It was my fault. 'Cause I killed one of his friends.

"Happened once when he was gone off somewhere. Gone for weeks. My mother left me in the car, parked on a hill. She left it running. Ran into some house to buy dope. I was, I don't know, four or five, maybe. I was standing on the seat playing like I'm driving. Steering the wheel. Turning knobs. Pulling stuff. And it started rolling. Backwards. The wheels must have been turned. The car rolled into the road. Not going fast. Mom and this guy came off the porch. She screamed. The guy, he came out in the street chasing the car. He looked like a cowboy without a hat. He was closest to the passenger door, so he grabbed the handle. Dug in his feet. Actually stopped the car rolling.

"I don't think I even saw what happened. I only know most of this from her telling it. When she got drunk. Like it was my favorite bedtime story. I do remember hearing brakes. A car hit our car on the passenger side. I flew across the seat like the other car was a big magnet. Hit the passenger-door window hard. And I remember. When I flew at the window? I saw that guy's cowboy shirt— buttons pressed all crooked up against the glass.

"Things were bad before. But after that? See, everyone knew. My father, he sometimes sounded like he was bragging on it. Like warning his friends—how his pissant kid had killed a man. But from then on I was nothing to him. Not even to knock me around.

"Mom. She caught it all. He'd be gone a week, or a month, then come back, all nice at first. For a day or two. Then she'd have to get away or wind up dead. She would just leave me behind. I would hide. But I was invisible to him anyway. He'd eventually leave. She'd eventually come back.

"Living with her? I was . . . tolerated, I guess. She worked odd jobs, mostly to buy dope. She'd fix food. For herself. I was on my own. I had to open cans from the cupboard to eat. I'd swipe money from her sometimes. Buy Frosted Flakes. Candy. If she caught me red-handed, I got smacked. She'd find places to hide her cash. When I got older, I stole from neighbors if I needed stuff. Sometimes kids recognized their clothes. We'd fight. If neighbors got mad, we'd move. Sometimes kids found out I was a killer. More fights. So it was okay by me that we moved a lot.

"Sometimes it took my father a while to find us. He always did, though.

"A couple times she moved during the day. While I was at school. I'd find her every time. I'd walk into the new place—some guy's apartment maybe. Another uncle. And she wouldn't say anything. It was just normal. Once it took me two days to find her.

"Sometimes I liked the uncles. But there were a lot of 'em. It was better if I didn't care. My father sometimes sent them to the emergency room. And we'd have to move again.

"I got to my fourteenth birthday. Don't even know how I knew it was my birthday. Probably a teacher said something. I got home. Waited for my mother. She's no sooner in the door than I took ten dollars from her purse. She yelled, but she wasn't smacking me anymore. I was too big. I went to the store. Bought a ready-made cake. In the parking lot, I ate it all. With my fingers.

"When I got back, my father was there after almost half a year. Jail time. He sat at the table grinning real big. He had Mom cooking a meal. Sit down with your old man, he tells me. And it was the first words he said directly to me since I could remember. Mom set three plates like Dad said. And he made us all eat together. I felt sick from the cake. But I ate.

"He went into a big speech about starting over. Blah, blah. He wasn't eating. Just drinking beer from a bag by his chair.

"And he had another bag of something. Put it on the table. Said happy birthday. I was surprised he knew. But I didn't move. Mom cleared the dishes. Ran water in the sink. Clattered stuff around. He said, well go ahead, open up. All smiles. So I opened the bag. Inside was a rubber baseball, a baby-sized vinyl glove, and a little wooden bat. The wood-burned label on the bat said 'Tiny Tot League.' 'Tiny Tot' was crossed out. 'Piss Ant' was scrawled over it.

"I just sat there. Convinced myself that not even for a split second had I expected anything else. Dad, he was rocking in his chair laughing. Mom said something I didn't catch. He stopped and looked at her. What did you say? She just kept washing dishes. Answer me! He got up.

Nothing, she said. But it was too late. He was behind her yelling, You can't even be civil enough to join the party. Here I'm doing my damnedest to make a new start. It's a joke, for Christ's sake. Look. Look at him. He gets the joke. Don'tcha boy? I should'a wrote 'Killer League.'

"Please go, I heard her say. Still working her hands in the sink.

"He turned on her. What? The party just started, darlin'. We got all night. Why don't you freshen up some? He put both hands on her shoulders. Pushed her face into the dishwater. She struggled, her hands on either side of the sink. Trying to push up. I could hear silverware being stirred around by her face. Saw the sharp angles of her elbows jutting up. Could see the bones under her skin.

"I stood up, the Piss Ant bat in one hand. Crossed the kitchen. I hit his back between the shoulders. He let her go. I connected again on the side of his head. He went down.

"Mom was catching her breath in deep sobs. Stepped over him, and ran for her purse. Then she was out the door. I followed her. In the car she was wiping her face on her sleeve. I climbed in. Uninvited as usual. She turned so suddenly to face me that dishwater in her hair sprayed me. What'd you do? she screamed. He's gonna kill you now. Kill me too!

"I wanted to say, What's new. We drove around for half an hour. Drove back by the house. His car was still there. Maybe you killed him, she says and goes, Oh, Lord! But fifteen minutes later we drove by again and his car was gone. We went in. Got some of our stuff. The Piss Ant bat was gone. She said things like, You gotta go. I can't have you here no more. We drove off. Drove around most of the night. Stopped at several ex-uncles' places. I waited in the car. She would knock on doors, talk, but no one let her in. Then, at one place a guy let her in. She didn't come back out. I slept in the car.

"Next morning? She came out. Said stay with him. Said, I'm saving your worthless life here. I got out of the car with a grocery bag of clothes. She drove off. The guy was getting dressed in a uniform. Had some papers in a briefcase. Said he was an army recruiter. It took me all of two minutes to realize—Mom signed papers to get me enlisted. Together they had claimed I was seventeen. Guy was happy to do the favor, in exchange for her night with him. He had quotas to fill anyway. I signed the papers. Why not? Figured it'd be like just another school. I was wrong about that. Anyhow, he put me up for a few days until I climbed on a bus to boot camp.

"Her idea of saving my life? She sent me to Vietnam."

34

Rat threw more wood on the fire, snapping my trance. I surfaced from his story. He had spoken very slowly, sentences broken by long pauses. At times I had thought he wouldn't continue.

The day had slipped into dusk. The far shore was barely visible through the rain. I had no idea what time it was. Something caught my eye in the water below. It rolled in the current and I saw a door. It was a garden shed washing downriver. This flood was definitely for real. The longer I looked away from the fire, the more I could see in the dimming light. The river was crammed with junk.

"Pretty bad, isn't it?" Rat was watching too. "I'm sorry I brought you here. Maybe you should go." He slid over to the entryway and looked down. "Well, maybe not."

I crawled over to see what he saw. The water was almost up to the lower platform. And running hard. I figured that made it ten feet deep at the base of the trees. I remembered feeling the current's strength when it was little more than four feet deep.

I did my best to keep the small sick feeling in my gut from becoming a crazy rush of panic.

"Sorry," Rat said again. He was saying that a lot.

This'll sound weird but—then we ate spaghetti.

"Hungry?" he asked.

Eating wasn't exactly on my mind, but he didn't wait for an answer. He opened a footlocker, grabbed the wire grill, two cans of Chef Boyardee spaghetti, and an opener.

I thought about Gramma Gram. When I was little and visited her house, she always gave me that same canned spaghetti for lunch. How was she doing? What was her emergency? For the first time I wondered how bad the flood was in town. Had it crested the levee? Were Mom and Dad still at the hospital? Had they tried to call me? Were the phones even working?

No one knows where I am, I realized.

I tried to visualize the motel, how the backyard sloped down through trees to the river. I froze, a picture coming into focus. There was no levee that far out of town. Rooms at the end of the driveway were lowest. They could be in water by now. My heart started thudding—the feeling I always got when I knew I'd screwed up in a major way.

But hey! Even if I *were* there, how could I save the motel?

What can one dork do against a flood?

I remembered the lone customer in his room. Was he okay?

Well, duh, Toddler! He'll just leave.

My inner thoughts were, for some reason, coming out

in Leaky's voice. That had to be a bad sign. Just kidding. Somehow thinking about Leaky was a comfort—something familiar in a world that had gone off the deep end. Literally.

The tremble in the trees from the hard-flowing water was something I had gotten used to. But I was sure it was getting worse. I looked around again at our small sanctuary. The deck was built on boards that spanned a space surrounded by three trees. The upriver side of the platform was attached to big limbs in the tree with the ladder. Downriver, the side facing the direction of Elmore, it was nailed into the branches of two smaller but good-sized trees. It was solidly anchored.

"Time to eat," Rat said.

I crawled back to the fire, using a scrap of blanket as a hot pad. Rat handed me a can of spaghetti. Gave me the one fork he had. He used a stick to gouge out noodles from his can.

We ate in silence. He seemed talked out. And I still felt battered just from listening to him.

"Good spaghetti," I said when I was done. The top half had been cold, the bottom scorched. But believe it or not, it *had* tasted great. Which meant I had been very hungry. Which told me it was later than I thought.

"Just like home," he said.

His words made me think of the scene he had described—eating from cans at the table with his mother. His was, for me, an unimaginable story. An unimaginable life.

While I had been thumbing through room registration

cards, thinking I was solving a murder mystery, Rat was listening to his shot-up father talk about killing Unk.

Last year, while I'd been writing a story about aliens doing experiments on motel customers, Rat was in Vietnam.

For *my* fourteenth birthday? I had a pool party.

Rat tossed his can into the river, pulled off the grill, and dropped his eating stick onto the embers. It was just enough for a few tongues of flame to reignite and throw some light around. The fire had nearly dried my shirt. I put it on, rolled my piece of blanket into a pillow against one footlocker, and lay back. Rat did the same.

The rain kept falling. In buckets. Cats and dogs. Strangled toads. The river kept rising. I couldn't tell if the night was passing quickly or dragging by. I had no sense of time except for the slow burning away of each stick Rat tossed on the fire.

My mind was going down crazy roads.

And Leaky's voice wouldn't go away.

Now what, Toddler?

It's weird. But I was just thinking . . .

That's weird, all right!

Just let me think.

Look! You can actually think without moving your lips!

Shut up! What I was thinking . . . you know how, in books, being a hostage is, like, an adventure? They're wrong. This sucks.

Hostage? What are you talking about? That rifle is

empty. Didn't you hear him? He said it took his father a while to die. Because he didn't have enough bullets.

Okay. But I'm still a hostage of the flood.

Oh, yeah. In that case, you are truly screwed.

Thanks.

Any time.

I was right, though. He didn't kill Unk.

You believe him?

Rat's not that kind of—

You actually believe a guy who just filled his own father with air vents?

I don't know what to believe.

Believe this. S-Y-K-O spells psycho!

Actually it's spelled . . . never mind.

That ticking time bomb? He just blew up, man!

But the guy, Rat's father? He needed killing.

What?!

The world's better off without him. Don't you think?

Who elected you God? Rat?

I don't know I don't know I don't know I don't know.

35

We talked once in a while. Mostly me. Once, I said I wished
I had my radio. That got us naming all the rain songs we
could think of, like "Who'll Stop the Rain" and "Listen
to the Rhythm of the Falling Rain." Rat remembered "I
Wish It Would Rain," by the Temptations. We sang the
chorus, which was all we remembered. "I know to you it
might sound strange, but I wish it would rain." It cracked
us up. I talked about movies, but Rat hadn't seen many.
Just those at the drive-in the last few months. As we got
sleepier we talked about any stupid thing that came along.
Rat asked if I had lived in Elmore all my life. I said I was
born in Albany. He asked if that made me an Albanian. I
said I might be an Albanite. He thought albanite was the
stuff they used to make bowling balls. I wondered aloud
why someone from New York City was a New Yorker,
but someone from Manhattan was not a Manhattaner
but a Manhattan*ite,* as I'd heard Gram call herself. Rat
answered sleepily, "Same reason if you live in Elmore too
long you become an El*moron.*"

At some point, out of the blue, I asked, "So, what was

Vietnam like?" He was quiet for a long time and I thought he was asleep. Then he murmured, "'Bout like this." I figured he was just dismissing my question. But then I thought about the rain. The dead guy. The fear. So maybe he meant it.

Finally, we just stared into the coals of the fire. Listened to the rising water. Waited for the night to end.

All nights end, right?

All floods recede.

All rain . . .

30

I jerked awake. A tangle of dreams slowly unraveled, leaving behind a smeary nightmare image of filthy red dishwater gushing from a sink, washing me away with hundreds of empty cans.

I'd been asleep? How was that possible? With the rain, and the constant creaking of the boards, and Niagara Falls roaring below, how had I fallen asleep?

I sat up. My bones ached from lying on bare boards. Rat seemed to be asleep himself. The fire was out. That's when I realized—I could see! The first light of dawn gave everything a dim, silvery color. Dawn! It was such a relief to see morning coming, I would have cheered if I wasn't so tired and sore.

I stood and stretched. Walked to the edge of the deck and whizzed, still marveling that I had slept. Rain pounded the tarps so loudly, I couldn't hear my own stream hit the river.

Something was wrong.

The trees still trembled from the water pushing against their trunks. But it was more pronounced. Irregular. And something else.

I abruptly came more awake when I realized—the deck was slanting. Not much. It was hard to tell. But I felt it when I shifted my stance. One foot was definitely lower than the other. And the tree I stood beside to take a leak— had it moved away from the deck? Was that four-inch gap there last night?

I took a half-step back from the edge, leaned out, and looked down the trunk. Protruding from the two-by-six deck supports I saw a couple gleaming bent nails reaching for the tree the same way I had when the river tried to sweep me downstream.

Then I saw something that made me wonder if I was still dreaming. The tree began, very slowly, to rotate.

"Rat," I whispered, as if yelling might make it worse. "Wake up!"

"I'm awake."

As I zipped my fly a low crunching sound resonated up the trunk. Thirty feet below, the base of the tree lurched downstream as if a rug had been pulled out from under it. The top of the tree tipped back toward me. The deck gave way. I fell onto my back, yelling something that was swallowed by an explosion of screeching nails and splintering wood. A dark mass of leaves rushed down over me. I twisted onto my stomach to cover my face. An incredible weight landed across my legs, but the deck continued to give, the angle steepening. Branches raked across the boards, dragging my legs over the edge.

"Todd!" Rat yelled.

I looked at him. He dove past the fire pit toward me,

one arm out. I reached. We grabbed each other's wrists. With nothing to hold on to, Rat splayed himself out flat. But still we slid down the steep incline of wet boards. The rifle clattered past us. My legs, my waist, dangled over the river. The tree pulled away. My chest slipped over the edge. The deck, released abruptly from the weight of the tree, bounced back some. The steel sink behind Rat, propelled by the bounce, tipped out from its hole. The remnants of our fire erupted into a powdery gray cloud. Searing orange coals showed themselves within the ashes and for a moment seemed suspended in the rain. The sink turned over and fell. Its lip edge caught the back of Rat's head with a muted *thunk,* then tumbled away. Rat's grip went slack in my mine. His weight slid against me. Amid a shower of burning embers, we fell.

37

I must have been screaming when I hit, because the river filled my mouth. It was bitter and gritty. Rat landed on me. It was loud underwater, a raging growl. Rat's fall twisted my arm behind my back and my grip on him almost slipped. I was pummeled by the current, quickly losing sense of which way was up. My survival impulse was to let go and use both arms to swim. But, for an instant, the thundering water sounded like the roar of a truck, and I remembered the pain of a bite, and saw myself letting go. Not this time. No matter how it hurt. Maybe Rat was unconscious. How would he survive? Instead, I reached back with my free hand and pulled him closer. Kicked madly. Broke the surface.

At first the current felt like hundreds of cold hands trying to grab hold as they rushed past. But we quickly picked up speed, flowing downriver. Abruptly we hit leafy branches churning in the water. Then we were turning. The pull of the current was suddenly stronger, sucking at me. A tree limb raked under my arms as if it were trying to break my grip on Rat. It lifted between us, taking skin off my wrists, rising. I clung to Rat's arm. To my amazement, we were lifted out of the water. I gasped for air. Caught a fleeting glimpse of an entire tree turning, trapped in a whirlpool at a bend in the river. Then I saw no more because the tree continued to turn and we were thrown free.

For a few seconds, a trick of the current pushed from below. I managed to pull Rat closer to me. Got his face above water and held on with one arm around his chest. But the position seemed to push me under. I had a vague memory of a whitewater canoe trip in Boy Scouts and a safety briefing beforehand. We were warned—if you fall from the boat, just go with the flow, on your back, feet first. So I got us turned, facing downriver, our feet leading the way. It seemed to work. The current gave us a little lift. I constantly had to fight with my free hand to hold that position. Tried kicking to keep my feet up, but Rat's limp legs were in the way. Quickly we reached the same speed as the river. The water around us was full of debris. For a couple seconds I glimpsed a cat not eight feet away, struggling to keep its head up. We hit turbulence. The cat dipped under and we went down too. When I splashed to the surface again and got Rat's head back above water, the cat was gone.

Ahead, a large shape loomed and I tried to make sense of what seemed to be rushing toward us. A house in the river. Misshapen, tilting crazily, water gushing into and out of broken windows. A corner of the clapboard-sided building parted water like the prow of a ship. I got a foot and an arm up to fend off the collision. We struck it a glancing blow. My hand made only brief contact with the house, but in that moment I felt the structure shuddering. Then we were buffeted away by roiling water and it was behind us.

I recognized where we were. We had just washed past Fischer's Bridge, or where the bridge once stood. Just beyond the bridge, the river churned wildly. I was spun around. Through the blurring rain I caught sight of the house again. It tipped. Fell. Rolled. The roof plunged into the river. The bottom of the house lifted out of the water. An entire wall peeled away and the building broke apart. Then we were sucked under.

I stroked with my free arm. Kicked. Pulled us back up. We went down again. And again. I was getting scared because I was getting tired, out of breath, coughing and gagging whenever we broke the surface. And I was scared because I hadn't felt Rat move on his own. How did an unconscious person know when not to inhale?

Just as I was resurfacing again I was smacked sharply on the back of my head. My face was pushed under. I kicked upward but hit something. Whatever it was, it was above me. I thrashed with my free hand and found an edge. Wooden. Pulled myself around it and up. It was a door. I struggled to climb onto it. With my sudden weight, the door's edge dipped sideways. We slid off. The door slid away. Out of reach.

I was exhausted but I lunged after it. My shoulders burned with exertion. I kicked furiously but my legs kept getting tangled with Rat's. I released his chest, shifted my grip back to his wrist so he was out of my way, then kicked desperately. Stretched. Slapped a hand onto the trailing edge of the door. Pulled it close. Carefully beached myself on the lower half, sliding my weight on gradually to keep from losing it again. I hauled Rat up, our legs trailing behind the improvised surfboard. With my free hand I clung to the doorknob. The door didn't hold us very high. But at least we weren't being sucked under by every little eddy in the current.

We rounded a bend in the river, and suddenly the horizon opened out into a flat expanse. There was no shoreline. The water simply flowed through trees. And among houses. The current slowed somewhat as the water spread to fill a wide valley—the valley that held the city of Elmore.

The city was neck deep in the river.

38

I laid my head on the door for a moment's rest in the somewhat smoother flow. Around me, rain spattering the floodwater sounded like applause. I almost didn't hear the shout. "Hey!"

I pulled myself higher on the door and looked around. Walton Street Bridge was gone. We were flowing past downtown. Rows of isolated brick islands were all that could be seen of the stores and offices along Water Street. They seemed to have turned their backs on me.

"Hey you! Hang on!"

Where was that voice coming from? In the wet gray light of dawn I saw a neighborhood of houses drift by. Apparently we had been pushed to the far side of the river. The nearest house showed only a roof and the top halves of the second-floor windows. Even with the strangeness of a flooded landscape, the guy standing on a rooftop looked odd to my exhausted brain. He waved frantically, pointing, his voice muffled by the rain. "Look out!"

I stared as if he was some kind of comical apparition, then it sank in. He was calling to *me*. I looked where he pointed just as the door lifted on a swell of water and smacked the side of a brick building. As soon as we stopped flowing with the river, the onrush from behind felt powerful again. It swept us off the door. I clenched Rat to my chest as we were hammered against the wall. With little strength left, I lost hold of the doorknob. Lost sight of the door. For a moment we were pressed hard against the bricks by the churning water that tried to flow around the obstruction. Then the swirling torrents peeled us away and pushed us along the side of the building.

One-handed, I grasped at the wall for purchase, digging at the masonry. We were dragged past a window that was a foot above the waterline—dragged toward the building's corner, the edge, the abyss, beyond which there was only more river.

I was tired. Too tired. Water was in my face, in my mouth. I knew Rat was submerged again. I could no longer haul him up without pulling myself under.

Through a blur of water I saw one last window sliding toward me. After that . . .

I groped up for the window ledge. Underwater, I pushed one foot against the brick to slow my slide. Got the smallest bit of traction. Water pushing at my back lifted me. Just a little.

I reached with my one free hand, as high as I could, swung wildly, hit glass. It didn't break. My fingers slipped across the panes, caught the edge of the bricks framing the window. My grip held.

My legs streamed ahead of me, battering against the

corner of the building. I felt the hungry pull of the river beyond. Water churned over my shoulders as if I was at the end of a rope pulled by a boat.

End of my rope. This what they mean?

With the building as an anchor, I hauled Rat up. Got his head out of water.

The voice again, very far away. "Hang on, kid!"

My grip felt slippery. I looked back at my hand. Blood streamed down my wrist from fingernails that had tried to gouge into brick wall.

I held on. Tried not to think about Rat. Couldn't tell if he was breathing.

Just held on. So tired. So heavy. My arms, shoulders, on fire.

Rat's head went under again. I couldn't pull up anymore. Nothing left.

Heard a clunk behind me. The purr of a motor. Craned to look.

Weird. A boat. Three guys.

Fishing in this weather?

They reached. Lifted Rat from the river.

What a relief—his weight gone. I felt light as driftwood.

It was okay. I could let go now.

Go with the flow, man . . .

Water swirled. Soothing my shoulders.

"Hey! The other one!" Motor revved.

. . . the river of life . . .

Rough hands grabbed, pulled at me.

Felt the hard edges of a boat.

Thumped onto a wood floor. Smell of gasoline and fish.

Some guy pushed on Rat's chest. Mouth-to-mouth.

Sudden shouts.

Tree branches, leaves. A loud *whunk*. Motor stopped.

The swirling stopped. Leaves covered us.

Motor wouldn't start. A guy cursed.

I smiled. Caught in a tree again.

39

I didn't recognize the emergency room. There were two hospitals in town. The one where I had gone for my rabies shots was close to the river. This had to be the other. Leaky would soon be so jealous because I got there by helicopter. Not that it had been a great experience. Everything seemed rubbery and confused—rain in my eyes, lots of noise, people working hard around me, urgent talk about Rat's condition. Now I was sitting, doing what I learned from Rat. Waiting. They still had him in the back rooms. Concussion, a nurse said. Needed X-rays.

There were enough other drenched people that I didn't feel too odd sitting in soaking wet pants. Someone had given me a dry shirt, one like the orderlies wear.

I spotted a nurse making her way toward me through the waiting room with a clipboard. She wanted answers.

When we had first arrived, a nurse tried asking me questions. But Rat was rushed past on a gurney and I went after him. They pushed through a pair of swinging doors. When I tried to follow, a guy said, "Wait out there. They need to talk to you." But I didn't go back to the nurse's station. I had no idea where questions might lead.

How did you end up in the river?

What were you doing out there?

Why?

Innocent or not, Rat could be arrested. I needed time to clear my head. I stood by the doors and worried about him for many different reasons. After an eternity my legs were ready to give out. My fingertips ached—someone on the helicopter had wrapped them in loose gauze, which was now bloody.

Nurses, patients, and orderlies had been rushing back and forth through the doors. Finally, I simply followed someone in and held my breath. No one said a thing. A row of treatment bays, some with curtains pulled, lined one side of a cluttered hall opposite another nurse's station. Two bays down, I found Rat. He was on his side, a monitor tracking his heart rate. A nurse was doing something to the back of his head.

"Is he okay?" I asked.

She looked up. I was ready to refuse if she tried to send me back outside. But she returned to her work. "The wound is clean. We've controlled the bleeding," she answered. "You the one that came in with him?"

I nodded.

"Normally stitches wait until after X-rays, but today's not exactly normal. Since the patient is awake and seems fine, the doctor went ahead and sewed him up."

"Eighteen stitches," said Rat.

"Hey, you're awake." I went to the side he was facing.

He asked quietly, "What's the most stitches you ever had?"

"Seven," I said.

"Looks like I got bragging rights."

"What hit him?" the nurse asked.

"A sink," I said before realizing it was exactly the kind of answer that could lead to more questions. She just shook her head—seemed both baffled and knowing at the same time.

"Coulda been worse," Rat said. "Coulda hit something important. Doc said when they found me, some kid was tryin' to drown me."

"Yeah, but I screwed it up," I said.

"Too bad. That was your last chance." I couldn't quite figure out what he meant.

The nurse stood, gathering her things. "I'll be back when they're ready for you in X-ray." She left us alone.

Looking up at me, Rat's expression came into sharper focus. All kidding aside. "About what happened? At the house?"

I nodded.

"You do what you have to do."

"What . . . what *did* happen?" I asked, afraid of the answer.

He rolled onto his back. Winced when his head touched the pillow. Pinched his eyes closed.

"How'd it happen?" I repeated, trying to ask without having to actually say it. He still didn't answer. So I had to simply say it out loud. "How, you know, did you . . . shoot him?"

I couldn't believe a question like that was coming out of my mouth. It was unreal. Normal people live their entire lives without facing a situation that called for the question: *How did you shoot your father?*

Rat's eyes opened. Many times before, I had seen him look past me, or through me, sometimes look at me and not see me. But now his gaze drilled me where I stood. "I wish I had."

"What?" My mind flashed to the rifle cradled in his arm when he had come up behind me.

He closed his eyes again. Seemed to sag into the emergency room bed. "She did."

"Your mom?" He didn't answer. "You . . . you didn't kill . . ."

"Oh, I killed him, all right."

My thoughts whirled, trying to make sense of what he was saying. "I don't understand."

"I told you!" he said, suddenly impatient. "I watched him die." My blank stare forced him to explain. "She emptied that worthless twenty-two of hers into him. It stopped him good. But it took a long time for him to die. I coulda easily gotten him to a hospital. But I just sat there . . . wishing I had one more bullet."

40

I believed him. I don't know why. It just sounded true. Horrible, bizarre, but true. I was so relieved, I felt like punching my fist in the air and yelling: *"YES-S-S! I KNEW IT!"*

Instead, I asked carefully, "Where is she?"

It took him a minute to pull away from whatever vision he saw behind closed eyes. "Huh?"

"Your mom. Where is she?"

"Drove off," he said. If I hadn't been looking right at him I wouldn't have seen the very slight shrug of his shoulders.

"I didn't see him show up. I was in the back, cutting that downed tree off the fence."

He spoke quietly. I pulled up a stool and sat close.

"I hear shots. When I get down to the house, she's leaving in the truck. Passes me in the driveway. Never slows down. His car's there. I go in the house and find him all shot to hell."

I shuddered, having my own memory of a head in the doorway. "And he talked to you?" I couldn't imagine something so creepy.

"Yeah, well, not at first. He was in her bedroom door-way. On the floor. Lot of blood. He must have cornered her in there. She kept the rifle by her bed. Probably just for him. When I found him, I figured it's time to move again. Packed my duffel bag and I was ready to hitchhike out of there."

That jolted me. If I hadn't gone out to the theater in the pouring rain, he would have been gone by now. I had been that close to never seeing Rat again.

"But first I get the rifle. Gonna carry it down to the river and throw it in. Then I remember his car. Dig in his pocket for the keys. He groans like he's waking up. Grabs my arm. Real weak. I stand up with the keys. He opens his eyes. Sees me and grins big. Blood in his teeth. I back off, wondering what to do. He calls me. Wants a drink—some booze out in his car. I just stand in the living room. Wait for some idea. He lifts his head to see me. But can't. That's when he starts crawling back down the hall. He's moaning and groaning. Saying stuff like, 'Hospitals were made just for situations like this.' He drags himself into the living room. Sees I'm not making any move. 'Cause I had my idea by then. To just leave him there. He swears under his breath a few times. I head for the door. He starts talking. About his jail time. How hard it was to find her when he got out. How he loves her and couldn't tolerate no more damn uncles. That it was time they start anew. That's exactly what he said. 'Start anew.' I listen to his garbage. His blood's spreading on the floor, so I just wait. Think-ing I was almost in the same boat. When I got out of the army it took me weeks to find her. I had nothing better to do. I remembered she has this one sister. They talk on the phone once in a while. Anyhow, what I didn't know? What he told me while he bled out? He said she's been going into town and seeing him. I couldn't believe it!

"How he told it, he comes into town, figures out the uncle situation, catches Unk alone one night leaving a bar. Kills him with my old Piss Ant baseball bat he still carried around. Finds one of those roads through the cornfields, like you showed me. Dumps Unk in the river. Leaves town."

I was stunned to hear that my stupid TV-show murder theory was almost exactly what happened.

"Oh, you know that hat you found? Unk was wearing it when he was killed. But it was mine. See, one day Unk snatched it off my head. Put it on. Said, 'Now *I* look like a baby killer too.' He yukked it up. I just let him keep it.

"Anyhow. Dear old Dad? After police get nowhere investigating, he slides back into town. Stays at your motel again. Watches us. Then he makes like he bumps into her in town. I can just hear him, talking sweet. And she buys it! Again! Of course he gets her all doped up. So she starts hanging out with him all over again. Spending nights in town with him. Stops showing up for work at the theater. Then same old story—Sunday she comes home all beat to shit. He comes by later and takes his little tour through the theater. Shows up again yesterday. Tries more sweet talk on her. Gets himself blown to bits.

"So I'm listening to all this crap. He's getting weaker. Talking becomes mumbling. I go out, get in the car. Smells rotten inside. Makes me sick. I figure I'd rather hitchhike." Rat smiled faintly. "Told you, I wasn't thinking clear. I decide to hide his car in the woods. My mother might as well have as much time as possible—to get farther away. He musta tried crawling out the door when he heard me crank up the car. Then I heard you calling. I couldn't get back to the porch in time to stop you from finding him.

"Then I didn't know what to do with you. I knew you had to go to the police. But I thought if we sat out there at the river a while, that would give her time to get some distance outta Elmore. I never figured on a flood.

"Remember what I said. You do what you have to do, okay?"

It was my turn to not answer.

"Okay?" he insisted.

I shrugged stiffly.

"Okay," he concluded, like everything was settled. Then he yelled, "Nurse!" I mean, he really yelled it.

She hurried in. "What is it?"

"Ma'am? Could you please look at my friend's hand?"

41

Once my abraded fingers, as they called them, were treated and the scrapes on my arms were washed and prodded, I was sent out to the waiting chairs. I settled in to wait for Rat to be X-rayed. That's when the admitting nurse noticed me. Now she was on one knee in front of me with a clipboard. Time for those questions I had avoided when we came in.

She took down my name and address on a form. Asked some medical stuff about me. When she got to the bottom of the page I thought she was done, but she pulled out an identical form.

"And the boy they brought in with you?" she asked.

"He's a guy," I said.

"Pardon me?"

"Not a boy."

"Sorry," she said softly. "Maybe you can help me get his paperwork started while he's being treated. What's his name?"

"Rat."

She glanced up from her clipboard, curious. I didn't elaborate. "What is your relationship?"

I looked at her blankly.

"Are you brothers?"

I thought about that. Answered, "A friend. Rat's what everybody calls him."

"So, what's his given name?" Her pen hovered over the form.

"I . . . don't know." I choked on my answer.

She stared at me a moment, then I watched her hesitantly write: "(Rat)."

"What about his family?"

"I don't know."

"Are they in town?"

I thought about his father, probably floating down the river by now. And his mother, driving away. "I don't know."

She gave up. "We'll talk to him later. Can I get you anything?"

"Coffee?" I asked.

She smiled. "Be right back."

"Lots of sugar," I called after her.

"Hey, kiddo."

I looked up with a start. I had been lost in thought, trying for about the hundredth time to picture exactly where Mom, Dad, and Gram might be. I knew there was no phone service. And the nurse hadn't heard anything about the other hospital. That's where they always took Gram.

"Sorry, didn't mean to wake you. But your eyes were open," the "kiddo" guy said. He sat three chairs over, but when I looked at him, he slid one chair closer. "I find it helps to blink once in a while." He hurried to explain, "I was watching you for a minute. You were staring a hole in the floor. Me, I was trying to decide if you're the kid."

"What . . . kid?" I was immediately on guard.

"You the one who saved that boy's life?"

"He's *not* a boy!"

"Okay, okay. Calm down. What do I know? I just hear things. Want another cup of coffee?"

I glanced at the empty cup in my hands, then back at him. He wasn't quite Dad's age, had wet hair, wore a wet T-shirt, wet jeans, and wet boots. "Who are you?"

"Okay, that's fair. I'm Wes. I'm with the paper. Actually, this was my day off. But, a flood! No way I could sit home. Story of the century for Elmore. Worse than the flood of '46."

I was so tired, and he was talking so fast, I struggled to make sense of him. "The newspaper?"

"That's right. So, I been hanging around, hearing things. Heard about a couple . . . um, young men, who got pulled from the river. Heard one guy had basically saved his injured buddy. You know anything about that?"

I finally caught up with him. "You want to put it in the paper?"

"Could be. Depends on the story. Course, it doesn't look like the paper will print for a few days. Our building's in the soup. But who knows. We may get some press time from *The Herald* up in Watson Glen. Run off an emergency edition."

"You want to write a story?"

"That's the idea. Am I talkin' to the right guy?"

I shrugged. Looked into my empty cup.

"I thought so," he said without missing a beat. "You looked kinda shell-shocked. Got that thousand-mile stare like you just came out of a combat zone. Wanna tell me about it?"

I looked back at him. He gave an encouraging nod. I surprised myself when I said, "No."

Surprised him too. He pulled his head back on his neck like he thought I was crazy—as if to say, who in the world wouldn't want their story in the paper?

"No," I repeated quietly. "*I* want to write it."

42.

The reporter, Wes, was actually an okay guy. I told him my name and where I thought my parents were. Asked what he knew about the flood and about the other hospital.

Then we worked out a deal. I would write my story any way I wanted and he would insert it, whole, within his story. He insisted on standard editorial review for punctuation, that kind of thing. We would, as he said, "share the byline."

"This'll be cool," he said as we shook hands. "Kinda different. I like it. So, can you write? 'Cause I'm making a leapa faith here, kiddo."

"I can write," I said.

A couple seats over was his satchel. He pulled out a notepad and handed it to me. "I'll be back in two hours."

"You want me to write it now?"

"What? Something else you gotta do? Listen, this was your idea. We're not talkin' the great American novel here." He shrugged. "Look, if we do this now, we know it's a sure thing and everyone can relax."

I looked at the bandaged fingers on my writing hand. "I need something to write with."

He dropped a cheap ballpoint pen onto my lap. "I have some other stops to make. I'll be back," he said, dragging his satchel off the chair.

I watched him go. The coffee must have been working, because words were already coming to me. I peeled one of my bandages back. Taped the pen to my fingers for a better grip. And I started writing.

I was still doing some crossing out and rewriting when Wes returned.

"Whatcha got?" He sat down in a rush, freshly rain-soaked. I gave him the pad and he started reading. Even with my bad handwriting, made worse by bandaged fingers, he read very fast. At one point he nodded. When he finished, he looked up in disbelief. "You *can* write!" he said. "I can actually use this."

He stood, pushing the notepad into his bag, then reached out. We shook hands. "Watch for the next edition, kiddo!" He waved and disappeared.

I shook off the fog that always settles over me when I write. Stood and stretched. I looked at the clock twice to be sure I saw it right.

I'd spent three hours writing? Surely Rat was back from X-ray by now.

I pushed through the swinging doors. Someone else was in Rat's bed and I couldn't find the nurse who had worked on us.

I went to the desk. "Excuse me?"

A harried-looking woman turned. "If you're not a family member, you shouldn't be—"

"I wanted to know about the guy who was in that second bed over there."

"Are you his brother?"

"Yes," I lied.

"Where are your parents?"

"I don't know," I answered truthfully. "Stuck in the flood somewhere, I guess."

Her stern look softened somewhat. But she was not happy. "Things are bad enough. We don't need patients wandering off."

"What do you mean?"

"I mean, he was wheeled up to X-ray two hours ago. At some point he walked away. It's a mess. His admission forms are incomplete. I need you to answer some questions." She picked up the phone.

"Okay," I said. But I was backing away. Out through the swinging doors. Out to the waiting room. I knew then what Rat had meant when he joked about how I had failed to drown him. He'd said, "That was your last chance."

Rat was gone.

43

Snapshot: Me, waking to find myself sleeping across four waiting room seats and realizing it's the middle of the night, then sleeping on until morning.

Snapshot: Walking out into the rain, toward home, getting to the edge of the flood zone, helicopters crisscrossing overhead, people outside their houses, looking around, National Guard troops directing traffic, guarding stores with fixed bayonets.

Snapshot: Finding Leaky's house, not in the flood zone, but his basement full of water, taking off the hospital shirt and putting on dry, dry, dry clothes, his dad fixing eggs by heating the pan with a propane blowtorch, hearing rumors that a couple dead bodies had floated out of the morgue of the hospital where I knew Gram had gone, me feeling a sickening dread.

Snapshot: Realizing the rain has stopped, everyone outside, cheering, returning to the edge of the floodwaters, Leaky wading in to get a tin can of Charles Potato Chips bobbing in the water, me watching, determined not to get wet again. (We debated whether or not eating the potato chips constituted looting and decided it was unknowable. The chips were still crispy.)

Snapshot: Coming back to Leaky's house, finding Dad there and hugging for a long time. (He and Mom had been evacuated by boat from the flooded hospital to Irving High School. Mom helped there with emergency food preparation, while Dad came looking for me. He said Gram was fine, her intestinal emergency under control, whatever that meant. I briefly told Dad my tale, sticking to the truth but with gigantic parts left out, the same way I had written it for the newspaper. Dad returned to Irving High, telling me to stay with Leaky until he came back. Said we had to talk. Seriously talk.)

Snapshot: A new, sunny day, waters receding, mud and furniture everywhere, kids stacking derelict tables and chairs into fantastic forts for mud ball wars, the awful stink as Elmore begins stewing in the sun, mud turning to dust, leaving the same grit in my mouth that I had tasted in the river, finding the emergency edition of the newspaper with my story on page two, everything just like Wes had promised except for not sharing the byline—it was all mine.

Snapshot: Dad returning to Leaky's with Mom and with news that neighborhoods out near the motel are officially open for residents to return home, me finding the high-water line in my bedroom just two inches from the ceiling, Mom crying while peeling family photographs off the living room wall, Dad speechless about the mud, some places two feet deep—just shoveling and shoveling and shoveling.

Snapshot: Me sitting with my newspaper article, telling Mom and Dad everything. (Everything!) (Well, except for the cool box, which survived the mud just fine. And a couple other little things. Like the knife—you know, unimportant stuff. Believe me, I had lots of important stuff to tell. Two murders, for example.)

Snapshot: Me with Dad and two tired-looking policemen slogging through mud down to Rat's house, front and back doors wide open, mud stains up onto the roof, and very little left inside except mud. (The cops questioned me skeptically, took a few pictures, and said they'd call if they needed anything more. I sneaked a peek around back. My bike, of course, was gone.)

Countless snapshots: Of me, looking over my shoulder, thinking I hear Rat or doing a double take thinking I see Rat—and realizing I'm wrong.

44

It was a long summer. With lots of bright, sunny days. It's September now, and the motel is fully open again.

I wrote another story about the flood. About those guys in the boat who pulled Rat and me out of the water. I tracked them down and asked a lot of questions. Gave them my most heartfelt but hopelessly inadequate thanks. I personally delivered the story to Wes. He printed it! Then, unbelievably, he offered me a job, a regular column to share in rotation with eight other contributors. It's called "Around Town"—all local interest stories.

I'm actually getting paid to write!

For the newspaper job, I needed wheels, so Dad loaned me money for a new bike.

There were a million reasons for Mom and Dad to be angry with me. Going out to the theater while they were at the emergency room was the big one, even though I argued that the motel flooded too. I would have been forced out into the streets anyway. Nevertheless, all summer I was restricted to the motel, leaving only to conduct interviews for the newspaper, to visit Gram, and to finish my rabies shots, and for church.

Fine with me. When I wasn't doing clean-up or painting cabins, all I wanted to do was write. I got fast at hunt-and-peck on the office typewriter. Pages stacked up until it looked like a book. I was able to salvage stuff I had written before the flood by drying out pages from my old note-books and copying them—things like getting bit by the pup, and the story of how Leaky got his nickname.

Leaky was allowed to visit. He proved to be such a willing helper with motel repairs that Dad started paying him! And me too, believe it or not. Finally! Leaky also read my chapters as I wrote them, making sure he got lots of coverage.

Gram's in a nursing home and I visit a couple times a week. All summer I read to her from my story, not that she understood. But I could tell she liked the sound of my voice. Plus, reading aloud helped me hear and recognize parts that could be improved.

I was allowed to ride my bike out to the drive-in. To officially quit. Mr. Huber insisted on paying me for the two measly nights I worked. Because the theater is situated on somewhat higher ground, it suffered only minor flood damage. The wind on the day before the flood had been more destructive. They reopened quickly, but I haven't been back.

That same evening, after leaving Mr. Huber's office, I turned down by Rat's old house. No one had bothered to work on it yet. Inside, the mud was hardened. There was no trace of anything. I trekked down to the river through the mud-caked woods. Almost didn't see the crap-green car. Driftwood, debris, and dead weeds had washed up against it and over it. The cops hadn't even seen it from the house. Tangles of the same kind of debris had piled up around the bases of most of the trees. At the river, now peacefully within its banks, only the tree with the two-by-four steps had survived, some of its roots exposed by the hole where the other trees had been swept away. Many of the steps were gone and a few two-by-six supports were all that remained of the top deck.

I keep waiting for news that a shot-up body has appeared somewhere downriver. Nothing. Like it never happened. One day, someone will stumble on an arm sticking out of the mud—a fisherman, or some poor kid, will find it. I just hope it's not me. Though I admit—the couple times I've gone down to the river since the flood, I can't help but look. If a body shows up, then maybe the police will remember being taken out to a muddy little house by the river.

Writing all this down has been a way to keep Rat around. It was such a brief time that I knew him. And so much happened. So much that I haven't found words for yet, even after writing hundreds of pages. I don't want to stop writing. Because these pages are about all that's left of him. Sure, I have the hat and the knife in the stash box, wrapped and hidden in my closet. But Rat only comes alive for me in my writing.

I wonder where he is. Wonder if he's looking for his

mother. If so, and I know this sounds cruel, I would like to ask him why. I don't imagine he'd answer me. I know now that some things people do are impossible to understand unless you've lived their lives. Even then, most of it will never get told.

I wonder if he'll ever come back through Elmore.

What would be the sequel to *Rat Life*?

Anyhow, for my next "Around Town" column, I'm going to find the one-legged guy, Flipper. Ask him about Vietnam. I want to write that story now. I'll do my best to get it right. For Rat.

School will be starting soon. Still no report cards from last June—because of the flood chaos. So maybe it's not too late to improve one of my grades. This afternoon Dad's letting me take this story to Mrs. Hagerwood. I really want to know what she thinks. But first, I need a good opening line.

The End

Dear Dork,
The sequel would be called <u>Leaky Life</u>, obviously!
Your pal, Lee

"One of the true secrets of the Vietnam War—indeed of most wars—is the number of underage boys who enlisted using false identification, sometimes with the knowing consent of their parents. The number of underage soldiers who died in Vietnam is also unknown. At least five of the men killed in Vietnam are known to have been under seventeen years of age. One, a Marine, seems to have been only thirteen."

Dirty Little Secrets of the Vietnam War
James F. Dunnigan and Albert A. Nofi
(New York: St. Martin's Press, 1999)

AUTHOR'S NOTE

RAT LIFE *is a work of fiction. While I hope readers from my hometown of Elmira, New York, will recognize similarities to our actual city and its catastrophic flood in 1972, I also hope they will forgive any liberties I have taken with the city map and details of that tragic event.*

I wish to thank Drs. Kenneth Herzl-Betz and Randy Weidner for so freely sharing their knowledge of rabies treatment in the 1970s, and Dr. Timothy Bernett for help with emergency room procedures. If there are errors in this text, they are of my own making.

A big thank-you goes out to Gary Grace for his hands-on introduction to the rich Native American history in our Chemung River region.

To Aric Brown, manager of the Elmira Drive-In Theatre, a tip of the hat for an informative tour—and with special consideration for the theater, I repeat, Dear Reader, this is a work of fiction.

Last but most of all, I owe a deep and heartfelt thank-you to my first reader and most trusted critic, my loving wife, Carol, for enduring countless random brainstorm outbursts and seemingly endless manuscript readings.